infinitesimal

infinitesimal

hanjing wang

gatekeeper press
Where Authors are Family
Tampla, Florida

This book is a work of fiction. The names, characters and events in this book are the products of the author's imagination or are used fictitiously. Any similarity to real persons living or dead is coincidental and not intended by the author.

The views and opinions expressed in this book are solely those of the author and do not reflect the views or opinions of Gatekeeper Press. Gatekeeper Press is not to be held responsible for and expressly disclaims responsibility of the content herein.

Infinitesimal: And Other Stories

Published by Gatekeeper Press
7853 Gunn Hwy, Suite 209
Tampa, FL 33626
www.GatekeeperPress.com

Copyright © 2023 by Hanjing Wang

All rights reserved. Neither this book, nor any parts within it may be sold or reproduced in any form or by any electronic or mechanical means, including information storage and retrieval systems, without permission in writing from the author. The only exception is by a reviewer, who may quote short excerpts in a review.

Library of Congress Control Number: 2023933447

ISBN (paperback): 9781662933721

eISBN: 9781662933738

Contents

Infinitesimal	1
To Each of Covered Imperfections	15
Collision Theory	29
Biscuits & Rain	41
Criminal #1240	51
Sacrifice	65
Counseling Core	75
Immortals	87
The Heaven Express	101
Dowager	115
Day's Dozen	125
Sunlight, Seawater, Saliency	137

Infinitesimal

In a town between two mountains so tall they block out the sun, even birds only reside as visitors, wings already flapping to continue the annual journey south; yet humans stay, and they stay for generations upon generations until the children's feet are permanently stained brown from dirt and the wooden walls of houses are so faded in color they seep into the scenery like too-watery paint.

My ancestors refused to move, ultimately forcing the outside world to move for them. Eventually, it does, and each year the country's third best university flips through chalky applications to accept one—precisely one—student from the town. In the past, they used to study law, then literature, then business, then physics, and now computer science; the carriages and horses gradually became metal shells with engines. What remain unchanged are the cries of joy from one household every first of May and the car that disappears between the mountains, accelerating at an almost linear rate, promising never to return.

Here, surrounded by wisteria and neighborly gossip from everyone else who never leaves, is where I came to be. But the spot, the acceptance letter, the beckoning music radiating from overpopulated cities—that is where I'm destined to go.

My father had never been second in his life.

He was the eldest son of an eldest son, always the first to run into a rocky creek or hand in his work on Monday mornings. Nowadays, he's the earliest to show up at ClearDays Bank, opening its rusty lock and turning on the air conditioner that always needed seven minutes of running time to cool the place before all the employees and clients arrived.

The only exception was arguably the most important one, caused by a particularly cold winter and a nasty season of pneumonia. Three fitful weeks later, my father was left with barely enough energy to lift his pens, a hastily written and dutifully rejected application, and a fact too sudden to wrap his mind around: he was stuck here for the rest of his life.

More terrifyingly, as the days dwindled into decades, he found himself getting a conventionally presentable accounting job, marrying a conventionally pretty girl who made delicious pickles, taking over the conventionally sturdy two-story house after his parents died, and going to conventionally filled churches on Sundays. His edges were sanded, he realized, teenage dreams snuffed out by mundane inconveniences.

So he made sure to set himself apart with the last flickers of defiance. He gave his daughter, me, a Christian name, when everyone else (except one family) named their children after folktale heroes or roadside flowers. He painted the kitchen tiles a glistening ivory and my room dark blue, the edges of my walls never even slightly fading in color with his regular checkups. And he made sure I knew that I was going to get out and fulfill what we had been set out to do, the only family in town with a private study—leave the mountains and etch my family name across the country, no matter the cost.

Math lessons from the day I learned to hold a pen and concentrate for more than half an hour. New notebooks every semester, even if there were no notes to be taken, as I learned to relax in the tangy smell of paper. Lights out at nine and curtains open by seven. There was no negotiable room, not for a family living on patterns and numbers inked neatly across refrigerators.

Somehow, I grew up to be anything but rebellious; or rather, I was rebelling against the mundanity of rebelliousness. My hands kept writing equations as red, itchy calluses formed. I wore clean yet laughably unfashionable outfits to school. I even followed the sleep schedule for a period of time—that is, until I turned eleven.

Perhaps the reaching of an age represented by a number with no divisibility rules reminded me that life was, at its core, unpredictable. Perhaps my father and mother decided to also retreat early that night, the whole house unusually empty of quiet chatter and scribbling. But no matter what, I opened the small window right beside my desk and climbed out, bare feet hitting on stone pavement and hair puffed by wind or momentum.

And that was how I found another girl—or rather, how she found me, panting from the unaccustomed exercise and nose tip slightly red from the autumn chill. I stopped by a redwood tree to catch my breath, expecting anything but a voice to call me from above.

"So I'm not the only one."

The voice was like mulled wine, something I had never heard before, and so I looked up. Nestled in between baring branches, there she was—flowery skirt and sweater with knits so obviously messy yet filled with love, eyes so gray they burned like ash. I knew her name then, its presence on the tip of my tongue, before she uttered it.

"I'm Jane."

I knew I had to introduce myself too, but it took me three solid seconds before I was able to formulate presentable words. "Hi, I'm Sophie."

She smiled, as if the peculiarity of my name was endearing. "Sophie, the view up here is spectacular."

If I had been any more rational at that moment, I would've questioned how far one could see in a cloudy night, or how elevating your height by a few feet did virtually nothing if you planned on observing the stars from an improved angle. Yet, I simply climbed.

She was right—at least, I believed her, and that made what I saw better: the moon lit up one of the mountains, its peak glowing like a lighthouse that drew me away from my ocean-blue bedroom. The air was clearer up there too, leafy scents covering sublunary odors of pot-braised pork.

I don't recall what we said that first encounter, nor did I stay for long: the shadow of my figure was still slanted when I snuck back to my room, giddy with the teeth-chattering momentum of disobedience. That night, I dreamt of pale moons and lamp-lit floral patterns.

The next morning, if my mother noticed the mud on my cotton nightgown, she didn't point it out.

I began meeting Jane regularly as the seasons warmed, the redwood tree as our hideout. Initially, I'd go there every once a week, hoping to catch her billowing dresses in between growing leaves. After a few missed times, I grew tired and arranged an easy table of meeting times: every prime number, from 2 to 31, for every month.

She preferred to call it differently—an alignment of stars. As I would soon learn, Jane came from a family no less scholarly than ours, although they spent it on hardcover books and organic ink. Her name came from a foreign novel her parents found, when they couldn't decipher any words except the author's name on the front cover. And like my family shaped me in mathematics and sciences, hers shaped her in literature. She would often carry a half-filled black journal, hands scribbling away underneath flickering streetlights while waiting for me to show up.

Sometimes, I wondered if our stark difference made us somehow fuse together more naturally: I could comment on the Fibonacci sequence's effect on architecture, while she could describe the tilt of roofs so vividly I would know what it looked like with my eyes closed. She was everything my parents never taught me, the one piece missing in the beautifully constructed machine of a girl: art, poetry, and barely hidden revelations.

We'd talk about town—after all, there was nothing to talk about when everything surrounding you was barren land and mountains, the same people you've seen since childhood, too-sweet popsicles and more barren land. The butcher's daughter was to be married. The old couple by the creek planted a new tree outside their door. Twins were expected from two families by the end of March.

A few moments later (or maybe it was hours), we'd find ourselves drifting to different topics. Jane was well versed in English, her vocabulary far superior to that of our teachers. Sometimes, if she could, she'd find old texts in the town library and read them until she memorized each word, then recite it to me. I'd never been a diligent language student, yet the foreign syllables rolled off my tongue smoothly when following her sentences: Poe, Frost, Shakespeare.

Other times, I'd tell her about the math textbooks in my house, and which chapters caught me most off-hand: three-dimensional vectors, matrices, and trigonometric functions. While the town only had a few computers, my family owned one, so I knew about HTML or Javascript too. Once or twice, I could feel her breath slow down, eyelids fluttering as I rambled on and on about inverse equations.

"Jane?" I would whisper, careful not to disturb her sleep.

"I'm listening," she would answer, and I'd continue with an eruption of butterflies inside my ribcage.

Once, we tried reading a book together, Jane and I. Since reading itself was her idea, she allowed me to pick the book; I took one from my ninth grade classroom named *The Curious Incident of the Dog in the Night-Time*, as the protagonist's ability to memorize all prime numbers until 7057 fascinated me. We traded the book back and forth during our meetings, verbalizing thoughts.

"The metaphors are quite wonderful," Jane would say, pointing at an analogy of how prime numbers represented life.

On the other hand, I frowned at frivolous mentions. "What do you mean, one can never figure out the rules?"

"The author probably wanted to say that life is more than patterns," she answered matter-of-factly, already onto the next page.

"If you actually take out all patterns, what's left is an occasional natural disaster and erratic, brainless insects," I grumbled. "Especially in a town like this, everything is goddamn predictable. The only difference is if it's linear, or quadratic, or cubic, or quartic. Some might make you work a few more steps to figure out what exactly the pattern is, but it's there all the same."

Jane shook her head playfully, amused by my annoyance. "That's not true."

"It is, factually."

A few seconds of silence.

"Have you ever heard of the word *infinitesimal*, Sophie?" she asked so softly, I wasn't sure if I was meant to hear the question.

"Yes, once or twice."

"Doesn't it go against the rules we set up?" she pointed out, eyes fervent now as if preaching. "*Infinite* means endlessly big, so according to the rule of roots, the word *infinitesimal* should denote something related to enormity. Yet it doesn't. It means an indefinitely small amount, contradicting with part of itself."

Somehow, that statement angered me, whether with its logic or truth. "Something small can still lead to infinity, Jane. Like the harmonic series—you know it's diminishing, its terms approaching zero through increasingly tiny values, but the overall sum of the series still equates to infinity."

"That's not what I meant—"

"Your idea was based on a false premise." To this day, I don't know what made me say that, but it took effect on Jane almost instantly. She turned away, held-back tears glistening under the moonlight. I did not know how to comfort her; no one in our town did, preferring warm rice and folded bedsheets over apologies. So, stupid as I was, I awkwardly climbed down the tree and walked back home.

I fidgeted over loose seams for four days, but when the 17th of the month hit, she was already there when I knocked on the trunk slightly.

We did not pretend to know each other at school—she preferred to hang out with everyone during lunch, gossiping over the teacher's romantic pursuits, while I lounged in the edge of the cafeteria with a tin lunchbox and thick worksheets. Sometimes, our eyes would meet, and she would smile a little. I tried to smile back, in between question thirteen and fourteen of modular arithmetic.

Slowly, the meetings consumed more and more of my time. They often extended well past midnight, and the morning alarms did little to truly rouse me. I'd make it through the day with barely concealed yawns, watch my under-eye circles darken recurrently. Jane seemed to do the same, her hands propping up cheeks during breaks.

My grades also started slipping. The semester before applications, the 95s started to dwindle to 92s, then 90, then 86s. One time, my math teacher pulled me aside after class, nose scrunched and fruity perfume blocking my senses.

"Are you struggling with something lately, Sophie?" Her voice was too soft, too rushed around the consonants.

"No, I'm quite all right."

"Then why have the past few exams—"

"I'm working on it."

"Sophie, please." I was afraid to meet her eyes. "You have just a few months left, and I'd hate to see the former number 1 lose the opportunity given right to her."

Nothing came to my head but *Please don't tell my parents.*

She didn't have to—my chemistry teacher did, when I forgot how to order the groups in class. A quick note home, and I was standing in the living room, face-to-face with a suffocating fury.

"Eighteen years," my father muttered while pacing back and forth. "Eighteen years of the utmost trust, and this is how you repay us."

I did not dare to speak.

"How can you be so? After all your promises and your potential, you waste it on god-knows-what. Whatever you're doing is more important to you than your future? Than your parents??"

"Father—"

It was gone before I could comprehend—the sudden red in front of me, the loud cracking sound, the almost chilly pain that lingered on my left cheek. My father's two sunken eyes stared at me, as if he couldn't quite believe himself either, while my mother hurried to pull him away.

"There is no need, she is our daughter, after all—"

He seemed to compose himself at that and interrupted her. "I cannot make you do anything. But I will not watch you waste generations of hard work for a fleeting diversion. You will wake up at six from now on, and bring back your grades as well as draft your application like a proper student. Do I make myself clear?"

"Yes, Father," my voice came out cracked.

He slammed the door as he left, and my mother hurried after him, her footsteps a spurt of noise in deadly silence.

I looked at the calendar and realized it was February 23rd. Two weeks before my application due date, and a prime number. I sat in my chair until nine, where the house's lights turned off and I could see nothing but the waning moon outside. Forty-six seconds later, I was climbing out of the window again and running toward the redwood tree, feet moving faster and faster uncontrollably.

I knocked on the trunk. I glanced up. I whispered, "Jane?"

No one was there.

She might be late, I told myself and climbed until the branches split into twigs. Sitting there, watching lights flickering out the way I knew they would—the baker's first, then the library, then the grocery store, and lastly the restaurant—I started to estimate the number of seconds between each extinguishment. Five. Thirty. Seventeen. Sixteen.

I tried to find a pattern to it, mentally graph the results in my head. Would the function of best fit be a line? Quadratic? Exponential? Logarithmic?

Nothing. There was nothing to it.

So I stayed there until there were no lights left, grappling with the fact that math did not save me at all—nor did literature, or psychology, or biochemistry. How nothing seemed to matter in this world, the amount of prime numbers you memorized or the poets you can recite off the top of your head, if two mountains separated you from the rest of it. How the only way to success meant cutting off the only person I'd ever come to truly know, but the only way to contentment meant giving up future and whole versions of myself.

I thought and thought and thought, hardly noticing the sky brightening and the absence of a figure by my side. When I walked back home that day, two hours between treetop abstractions and early studies, a decision was already made.

Father and Mother didn't need to proctor me; for two weeks, I would return home from school, shut myself in my room, and study. I wrote my application in hour-long bursts, poring over phrases and words that would likely not matter in the face of grades.

Jane tried to seek me out a few days later, on the 30th. I had missed our meeting, and I knew she thought it was just an emergency. I was eating lunch, face buried in a review resources book, when she arrived.

"Sophie, how—"

"I'm good, thanks."

The indifferent words formed easier than I thought they would. I didn't glance up, for I knew I couldn't maintain my concentration if I saw her doe-like eyes brimmed with tears. A few seconds later, I heard fading shuffling and knew she headed back to her table with her plentiful friends and gossip.

She didn't attempt to talk to me again.

Days blurred into weeks into months. I don't recall much, except for the small sigh of relief when I submitted the application, the larger sigh of relief on May 1st when the letter carrier knocked on our door, and the large crowd that gathered to send me off. My mother wept in my arms—she was never good with parting with people, her daughter least of all. My father stood, tall and proud, yet turned away when I stepped into the car.

The inside of the clearly expensive SUV was comfortably chilly, and the rearview mirror revealed joyous faces that bled into one another. I prepared for a long ride ahead, a few hours of sightseeing, and eventually freedom.

And then I saw her. She wasn't smiling—didn't even try to attempt it. Her floral dress was more fitted, cinched in at the waist and flared at her hips. Her eyes, so used to holding tears, now held a sort of undisguised resignation that filtrated every inch of her body, from limp hands to messily rippling curls. For a moment, it was almost as if we locked gazes with each other. Her whole body stiffened, then her lips pursed as if telling me what I had realized myself.

You've failed. At what you wanted the most.

The car accelerated at an almost linear rate and the view turned to black as we disappeared between the mountains, promising never to return.

I love the city.

I love its bustling cafés and bustling people and bustling worlds that engulfed me, as if I was one of them. I love the newest versions of computers, thick books on mathematics, and iced coffee. I love my job as a programmer, but I love its pay more, money I can spend on hair treatments or nail polish or fancy French restaurants.

I love it so much that I rarely think of the town—except in two ways. Once every two months, I gather up a small portion of my pay as well as some interesting accessories and mail it back to my parents. It's part filial piety and part pride: Everyone must know their daughter is doing well, riches and knowledge oozing in ways the townspeople would've never imagined.

The other occasion is much less preferred. Sometimes, when I hurry down an unfamiliar boulevard or ride one more metro station than expected, I'll find myself underneath a redwood tree, its distinct tinge of sweetness coercing me to look up. There, in between thick branches and overgrown leaves, dappled sunlight comes through. If I pause long enough, two figures will start to take shape—one with outrageously ugly nightclothes and the other with handmade shirts, faces following the movements of constellations and hands not quite touching. My hometown, in the middle of cosmopolitan constructions.

I'll wait, to see a flash of gray or floral patterns. But the ephemeral light will change, and all I'll be left with is a slight knock of wood against my heart.

To Each of Covered Imperfections

My nail is slightly cracked.

Mother will be horrified if she knows—nose scrunched and permanently shaded brows turned to a frown—so I try to smooth over the otherwise clean edges, apply lip gloss to the one line of dark red in the middle of carnation pink. When that fails, I decide to just clench my fists and place them behind my back.

No one will find out.

They're waiting for me beside the front door; Daisy, Heather, and, of course, Mother. I see their outfits before I see them: a white square-neckline dress for Daisy's large eyes, rose crop top and skirt to bring out the color in Heather's cheeks, and a matching checkered suit for Mother. Two braids, slight curls, and a top bun. Coral, pink, and magenta lipstick. Waiting for a fourth figure to join them—an accessory that will soon become their counterpart.

"Iris!" I hear vaguely. *Not again.* Grabbing the leather purse Mother bought me a few days ago, I hurry down the stairs.

I must be walking too fast, because Heather eyes me disapprovingly. She always says that I look more poised and proper when I stroll with my hands clamped together, not running down the stairs with my half-ponytail already losing shape despite three layers of hair gel. But who can blame me—or any other sixteen-year-old girl today?

Certainly not her. She went through this three years ago, and Daisy two. I still remember how Daisy wore the wrong shoes and almost had a panic attack on the car ride there, or how Heather refused to go in before adding even more mascara. How they exited after the excruciating suspense with beaming eyes and navy ribbons.

Poise doesn't matter today behind closed doors; nothing matters except for The Refinement.

I kiss Mother on the cheeks from the corner of my mouth, making sure my lipstick does not smudge her perfectly polished foundation. I allow the chauffeur to open the car door for the passenger seat—my sole chance of sitting in the front before I turn eighteen, a singular presence about to confront a momentous day. The air conditioner is blowing directly toward my knees, which are bare and slowly turning pink under the chill.

"Tammington Hall, Elvis," I hear Mother say, even though the chauffeur already turned left toward the city hall. It's usually a ten-minute drive, yet today, cars in gray, black, and any other neutral color are barely inching forward on lanes in the middle of neatly trimmed shrubs. If I had taken my vintage Polaroid camera with me and snapped a picture, it would look just like the old movies from the early 2000s; oversaturated plants and clothes beside monotone houses and automobiles.

I expect Mother to make small talk (she always did), but instead she opens up her pocket mirror and checks her hair. Later, I know she'll be conversing with other matriarchs while waiting for my results, the hand around her coffee cup gilded with a solitary yet undeniably fluorescent taaffeite. On either side of her, my two sisters are busy with their schoolwork, one typing furiously on a laptop and the other buried in a hardcover textbook.

I attempt to distract myself by scrolling through my phone, but the elephant in the room is too demanding—more than a decade of preparation and bedtime stories culminating in a ten-minute examination that determines my societal placement. Under circumstances of major matter, silence is like confirmation of the worst; my family seems to be accepting defeat even before the actual event takes place.

"Mother," I ask, voice coming out shriller than I expected. She notices it too, and glances sharply up at me.

"Do not speak like that in front of the doctor, Iris," she warns, lips slightly pursed together in show of great disappointment. "Lower your pitch and talk slowly, or else he will not even so much as glance at you before deciding—I told you this a few days ago."

"Yes, Mother." Sounding better this time, I focus my attention on Daisy's dress; while still her classic shade of off-white, the lacy details today are in a floral pattern, delicately sewn to the rest of the cotton fabric. At someplace near her thigh, the end of a thread pokes out, its color slightly paler than the material around it.

I look away quickly, but Daisy has already followed my gaze, so she notices too. With almost unnatural fluidity, she shifts her dress so the thread is hidden from Mother's view. Then, using the tip of her yellow acrylic nail, she swiftly cuts off the thread.

Thank you, she mouths to me, then returns to reading.

"Iris," Heather mutters, face slightly blue from her laptop screen, "what do you reckon the other girls from your class will get?"

That grabs the attention of Mother, who is now looking at me expectantly as if I can perfectly recite every name of the girls in my grade—I can't.

But saying that will simply earn another disapproving look and a lecture on how carelessness means self-deprecation. So, I start with my friends, and pray their interest dwindles quickly. "Mollie will definitely be one of the Idealized, don't you think?"

Mother's gaze shifts slightly right—a sign that she's trying to recall Mollie's appearance and give her a number. My friend has auburn hair, long lashes, and an almost unrealistically curvy body, so I have no doubts about my answer. "You're probably right," she finally answers. "Continue."

"Maybe some will be Improved. Cassie?" As soon as I say it, I realize the wording error and fight the urge to clamp my mouth.

"Cassandra," Heather corrects with hands still on the keyboard, though she quickly scans Mother's face.

"Iris." Although said evenly, the words contain a warning coming from Mother. "Please be mindful of how you present yourself, especially today."

"Yes, Mother."

"Cassandra is quite pretty," Daisy cuts in, flashing a grin that shows exactly her eight front teeth. "I wouldn't be surprised if she's part of the Idealized too."

Heather rolls her eyes. "It doesn't matter if she is pretty. If she isn't perfect, she won't be an Idealized. Many of us are pretty, Daisy. Remember that girl in your class; Sara, I think she was called? One of the prettiest, and an attention grabber too, but she was put in the Improved pile. Because she wasn't perfect. Not a lot were."

She adjusts her hair slightly after the last statement, almost aggravated. Heather and Daisy were both put as Idealized, and so was Mother. They were all one of the two or three people in their classes to not have Changed at all.

"Whatever you say," Daisy responds mildly, "but I still believe Cassandra is beautiful enough to receive the highest rank."

"Are you saying she is flawless, Daisy?" Heather challenges, looking out the car window, eyes slightly narrowed.

"Perhaps."

"I just saw two large acne marks on her left cheek last night. They won't fade after just a few hours."

"And she is smart enough to add some concealer to cover up minor blemishes."

"Stop the childish bickering, both of you," Mother says, and my two sisters resume doing their schoolwork immediately, scratch marks forming on a page of Daisy's book as she grips it tightly. "No matter how pretty this Cassandra girl might be, she will not be as flawless as our Iris."

I shift uncomfortably, trying to not glance at the broken nail hidden in my fist. I think of yesterday, when I was laying out the pale violet chiffon dress for today, and realize I'm starting to forget the order of the periodic table. I must start reviewing when I return home today to prepare for next week's exam. But no matter how much I try, I still can't partially decompose a rational fraction.

"I have flaws," I say quietly, well aware of the surprised reaction Mother will give me. It seems downright narcissistic to accept such a hyperbolical compliment, especially when I am set to be assessed in a few minutes.

Mother sits a bit straighter and stares straight into my eyes. She has a wrinkle forming underneath her right eye, and no matter how many layers of foundation and powder she adds, it still remains visible if you squint hard enough.

"Iris, you are flawless. You come from a family full of objectively flawless people, and you've been flawless ever since the day you were born." Her tone is lovingly final, unaccepting of any rebuttal, yet I give some all the same.

"I'm not though, Mother." Subconsciously, I touch my nose—a horrid flat thing that looks laughable next to my sisters' sculpted ones. A sure symbol of unattractiveness.

"You are, and darling, you have to be. Saying, believing, and acting as though you are anything less is detrimental to your self-worth. We're only at the prominence we are now because we are perfect, and because we believe that we're perfect. Do you not understand? Do you want to see our values crushed to the ground?"

I avoid her pressing gaze and look at my waist. Under the tight dress, it is about to either burst or block all incoming air. "Can we not just accept our flaws and still be powerful, Mother?" I know that I am only repeating the same line of reasoning I've been saying my whole life, and I can almost say her response for her—the same verbose lines I've received between seventy-five-minute classes and playground frolics, seen tucked inside novels and heard during televised debates.

Patriarchy. "That was what the patriarchal society thought centuries ago, and those very flaws were the deciding factors in shaming women." *Self-actualization.* "And only through the process of self-refinement and self-actualization did women achieve the social standing they have right now, Iris." *Ruin.* "The moment we stop being flawless is the moment we admit that we are less able than men and the moment men have justification to ruin what we own. Who we finally can be. Iris, how can you be so selfish and blind? And right before The Refinement too, when your perfection is finally about to be recognized?"

She stops for a second, taking a slow breath. Heather and Daisy shift in their seats, eyes still glued to their respective study materials. Only by glancing down do I realize that I had been clenching my fist for the past few seconds. The nail's crack is even more visible now; I hide my hand in the pile of fabric on my lap.

Mother does not continue. She simply stares at me, steady and almost peaceful but unwavering.

I think of disagreeing with her even more. I think of telling her about the boys in my kindergarten class who stepped on my fingers and never apologized because I never asked them to, the science exam I failed and forged a signature on during eighth grade, the smudged lipstick on my first night out. How these things do not make me any less good or worthy of a woman. I think of revealing my chipped nail and saying that its throbbing pain corroborates precious transience, its defect actualizing beauty.

"Tell me you are a feminist, Iris," Mother says. Tammington Hall's white pillars are visible in the window.

"Of course, I am, Mother."

"Then stop listening to your misogynistic voice and strive for perfection."

The chauffeur pulls the car to a stop. I do not have a chance to answer Mother before my door is opened and I step out into the blaring sunlight, the reflection of my diamond necklace creating trifling rainbows on the glass window.

The line is already visible when we step into the grand hallway. Dozens of girls stand in a neat row, their exquisite dresses looking slightly out of place amid marble and stone. To the side, family members wait near the exit, where their girls reappear with either a blue or yellow ribbon on the left of their chests—right above their hearts.

"Good luck," my two sisters whisper almost simultaneously. My mother merely nods, and before I realize, I'm left alone at the end of the line.

"Iris," says the girl in front of me, and I realize it is Ruby. We're not close in class but have always been friendly. "Aren't you excited?"

"Very." I plaster on a smile and hope the unwilling lift of my lips is convincing enough to prevent further questions. Mother's words still circle my head, waves crashing against rocks; I don't know what is more likely, evaporation or erosion.

"Well, I assume we're all going to get Improved, so what's the worry," Ruby continues, then lowers her voice. "But what if, you know, *that* happens?"

"That?" Pretending to be confused, I take the opportunity to scan the crowd. All the girls exiting have yellow ribbons, their family already leading them to the next room on the right. Not a blue in sight yet, and not a red either.

If we will get any red at all. Impossibles are hard to find.

"If someone gets deemed unfixable. What will happen then?" She seems earnest.

"I have no idea; my mother never told me," I answer genuinely. One does not talk about the Impossibles on most occasions; mentioning them brings bad luck, and I doubt anyone knows where they are anyway.

Ruby shudders. "Neither did my mother. Oh dear, I do hope all of us at least pass through with a yellow ribbon."

"Don't worry, Ruby. I'm sure we will."

My tone must have been final, or Ruby is too wrapped up in her thoughts—a welcome thing, since I am lost in mine as well—but we stop making conversation for the rest of the wait, only wishing each other luck when she is finally called in. I glance at the clock, which points to a time around noon. They must have set the room temperature low, because my fingers are ice cold when a middle-aged woman opens the door, her black hair in a tight bun and white robe clean of dust specks.

"Ms. Iris Edwards," she calls out, voice deprived of any ups or downs, and turns back in without a glance at me.

I quickly follow her, catching a glimpse of flashing yellow and Ruby's frizzy hair before the heavy metal gate closes behind me.

What unfolds in front of me is another narrow hallway, this one covered in gray tiles, leading to a second door. A plastic sign is glued on the front, black letters spelling out "DOCTOR'S OFFICE."

The woman opens the door for me, and I barely have time to walk through before it swings shut, the momentum pushing me further in.

"Hello, Ms. Edwards," says the man in front of me. He appears to be in his forties, hair slightly thinning and shallow lines across his forehead, yet he gives off a lively energy in the midst of a pristine room smelling strongly of detergent.

"Good morning," I say, praying that the clock has not struck twelve yet. Taking his smile as a sign, I sit in the chair facing him, just half a foot between us.

"Welcome to The Refinement, Ms. Edwards. I'm sure you've been looking forward to this since you were young." He examines me with his turquoise eyes, the color a bit too saturated to be natural.

"Of course, Doctor . . . Harsley," I answer, relieved that a name tag is clear on his vest. "I am very excited to get started."

He smiles, and without another word, takes out a small white device from his pocket. No larger than a phone, it seems to be a scanner and contains several switches as well as a few holes on the side facing me.

"Let's do it then, Ms. Edwards." He presses a button.

At once, three red laser beams fly out of the holes. I almost shut my eyes in horror, but then I realize they do not hurt to look at. In fact, it's enthralling to watch them twirl around my body, measuring and deciding silently. I can almost feel the soft lines graze my face in its bumps and turns, curling over every inch of my flesh.

Seconds may have passed, or minutes, or even hours. Yet after some time, the beams retreat back to their source, and Dr. Harsley stares at the screen intently.

For a few moments it is almost as if the world forgot how to breathe. Everything becomes static: The wind no longer exits the air conditioner, the noise outside reduces to silence, and everything waits in anticipation before the ticking device.

I know something is wrong when Dr. Harsley's left eye twitches a little. The result is supposedly out, judging by the absence of sound from the device right now. Yet he pauses several moments before looking back up at me.

And I see.

I see Mother smiling at me when I got my first piano test result. I see Father's postcards on his business trips to Europe. I see Heather and Daisy, still seven and eight, fighting over who was the doctor and who was the nurse in our games.

"Ms. Edwards."

I see Cassie and Mollie running toward me, flowers in their hair and clothes caked with dirt but we didn't care because it was middle school graduation and we were finally close to moving out—being adults.

"I have bad news for you, I'm afraid."

I see the old lady from the sweet shop, her back a bit more bent every time I visit her. How I promised her yesterday I will buy some more licorice next week. How she calls me "honeypie."

"You've been placed in the Impossible category."

I see and I see and I see. I see the past month, year, decade in front of my eyes. From my blurred peripheral, I notice Dr. Harsley smoothing out a wrinkle on his shirt before he presses another button on the device.

Immediately, three officers rush in, white robes blending into the walls as they inch closer. I try to hold on to the smell of Mother's hair right after a bath or the texture of Mollie's velvet hair ribbons or the taste of painfully sweet candy.

They touch me. I can feel them hoisting up my arms and pulling me from the ground. Dr. Harsley's voice echoes in the back of my skull, too narrow and too unclear for me to catch holistically.

"Ms. Edwards, please cooperate as we take you to your destination."

He mutters a few words at the end, most likely assuming that the rustle of cotton fabric and the bruising agony of elevation will drown them out. I hear though, more distinctly than anything he said before, "Someplace where we won't have to ever see your face again."

One of them tries to take my hand and I instinctively slap it away. They try again, using more force this time, and I last two seconds before my fist is torn open into five limp pieces of flesh; the broken nail is unconcealed now, its crack catching the ceiling light and giving the room a maroon glow.

"I'm sorry," I manage to whisper before they march me out and a perfectly black void fills my mind.

Collision Theory

[one]

The clock chimed half past four when the front door opened, prompting windows to shut themselves and wrinkled tablecloths to unfrown. Two quickly browning leaves attempted to sneak past the doorframe yet were decidedly ushered out by a no-nonsense click.

In came a singular gust of wind and a more singular man, heavy leather boots leaving faint dirt marks on the once-seamless tiles. A close examination would reveal just the right amount of stubble and short breaths with a hint of stale cigars.

If Nancy were to meet him in her youth—uncomfortably silky dress and mud-smeared cheeks and all—she would assume him to be her father's coworker; perhaps even his manager. She would curtsey slightly and mutter out a few monotonous compliments and pray that her mother would end up chattering instead of her.

She had been told recently to not look particularly young anymore; skin, like the slightly dusty grapes she stored in the kitchen cabinets during spring, became no longer desirable with scrunches and inky dots and fingerprints of time. "Herbert, darling, welcome home," she instead gasped, and rushed forward to take his coat with full knowledge that he would shrug off her flour-caked hands. They stayed like that for three seconds—two strangers who kissed each other good night yet never bothered to know what was on the other bedside table.

Herbert hung up his coat as expected and pecked her cheek. "I smell carrot cake," he remarked good-naturedly as he entered the kitchen, hands in pockets as if the half-cleaned pots would arrange themselves without any contribution on his end. Carrot cake it was—the almost too vibrant ones you see in televisions with big bubbly letters spelling out some cheesy phrase. "A carrot to carry it." "Carrots browned in Levittowns." So absurd they'd be realistic; so obviously fleeting she could almost grasp it.

Sighing, Nancy grabbed a glass bowl still stained with cake batter and began to wash. On the other side of the counter, Herbert lingered for a second before pouring himself a cup of ice-cold water and taking a big gulp before continuing.

"Don't bother with cooking today. We have a gala to attend."

"A gala?" she repeated, almost certain she was so absorbed in her childhood memories that the previous words were just an illusion. Galas (or parties, more commonly called) were so common in her early childhood; in fact, they were all she remembered: the earth-shaking laughter sneaking past her bedroom door, the paper wrappers clinging onto her curly hair when she had to get dinner, and the stench of alcohol radiating from damp couches the next morning. Nowadays it was more of sipping teas at pristine cafés and inviting her friends over for a few French-imported desserts.

"Yes," he answered, voice slightly clipped as if Nancy was being slightly dense. "Our firm is holding a formal dinner tonight, and many investors will be there. So will some from . . ." A wave of disdain. "Hollywood."

She knew his sentiment toward Hollywood, always wrinkling his nose at its mentions—he thought it messed up the edges of their tidy lifestyle and worried of its looming influence on their daughter, Connie. "Well, I guess we can just steer clear from them. I'm sure there will be enough people to socialize with."

He shook his head, fingers pressing down on his forehead; a classical picture of a troubled man, straight from the Metropolitan Museum of Art. "They're the best investors there, Nancy. I have to strike a deal with at least three, or else my sales record won't look great this year."

And she knew what he wanted her to do without him even opening his mouth. The same thing he asked for in corporate dinners or photos or every morning at the doorstep—yet a little more glamorous. The same role as his sturdy handbag and wool coat—yet a little more devoted.

She pictured herself yet again trying to navigate the hidden yes's and no's from the angle of her husband's nods, whiffing the stale scent of the latest perfume as she collided gently into yet another wife of a potential investor, clinging onto coarse suit fabric like an exquisite doll that was bought and marveled at but never enlightened.

"Honey, do be good today," Herbert said, and that was that. He never said his exact expectations out loud, but somehow Nancy always knew; or rather, she slowly figured her way out after unremarkable failures accompanied by unremarkable bruises along her wrists.

Only one concern remained.

"What will we do about Connie and David?" she asked, realizing that she was still scrubbing the now spotless pot vigorously. The cleaning sponge was digging into her fingernails like annoyingly blunt needles.

He didn't even look up from the thick booklet he was reading. "I'm sure the Marshalls will take them in, don't you think?" he muttered and flipped another page.

By "Marshalls," Herbert meant Mrs. Marshall, a recently widowed woman who lived two houses to the left and loved David's toothless laugh. She regularly sent them delicately baked sweets and offered to take care of the children, yet Nancy never took them to her house. She felt slightly shameful, given her sole reasoning was based on her friends' whispers about withering old ladies without husbands.

"Brilliant," she replied sheepishly. As if on cue, her apple-shaped timer rang, and she took the opportunity to let out a breath as heat whiffed out of the oven. *Lady's Home Journal* always recommended a minimum of fifteen minutes before taking cake out of the mold; right now, however, her brain was filled with half fleshed-out plans—ones that *Lady's Home Journal* would certainly discourage and couldn't actualize without her husband.

"What exactly do we need today, Herbert?" Nancy asked, hoping the slight flutter of eyes and lilting tone would showcase some degree of innocence. Yet the man in question merely continued browsing through his files.

"No need for you to worry about. Just charm them as you always do."

They'd had this conversation many times, many days, many different ways. So often, in fact, that she could almost recite it line by line; so frustrating that she never stopped herself from trying just once more.

"Honey, you can tell me anything, you know—"

"It's business, Nancy. You don't know and you don't need to know about business or politics or anything we're going to talk about—"

"I read the news, Herbert. I know about Eisenhower's policies and the war and—"

"Everyone knows about that, what we're trying to get here is jargon—"

"I've also read the books in your study. I know—"

"Reading books don't make you qualified, darling—"

"Herbert—"

"*Enough.*" She knew the rise in voice, the forming lines between eyebrows, the shift in atmosphere as if air suddenly became smog—blurring her vision and stopping her inhales. "I need a beautiful wife by my side tonight to show Hollywood what we have and how exactly valuable we are. A woman, not a politician."

Herbert pressed his temples, leaving two angry marks. "Leave the carrot cake and get ready. We'll leave at quarter to six."

With that, he mustered enough strength to tread up their wooden stairs, the abnormally loud noise somehow migraine causing. A dull pain from the tip of her fingers made her realize that she was still clutching onto the sizzling mold.

And in a pile of gingham aprons, messily thrown booklets, and overbaked carrot cakes, Nancy Periweather wished with all her might for her world to collide straight into hell—leaving behind nothing but equal-sized ashes.

[two]

"The limousine is coming in thirty minutes, ma'am," the doorboy's voice traveled faintly through wood. Rosalyn knew he wouldn't dare to open the door and say it directly. Seeing a woman partially undressed—and a famous one at that—took either overpowering lust or liquid courage.

She sure wanted the latter today, she thought, as the look started putting itself together: the blue chiffon with the gold necklace with the impossible heels. The papers might praise her for her ability to woo half of the acting industry or break the audience's heart with her perfectly heart-shaped lips drooping, but her real talent was color. Different patterned dresses and bold furniture and saturated paint strokes—she lived in the middle of it, savoring every last difference in hue and every collision of juxtaposing brilliance.

Of course, the public wouldn't know. What they also failed to notice, apparently, the papers still boasting about her latest polka-dotted skirt, was Rosalyn's steady decrease in screen time throughout the past five years accompanied by appearing only in suburban family advertisements and flyers selling kitchen appliances.

She knew, back in buzzing restaurant shifts where older actresses stressed over every carbohydrate, that turning thirty would mean many things. Wrinkles. Aching knees. Slightly rounder waists. But she never knew just how detrimental it was to her career and the one thing keeping her life afloat.

No, she didn't care about love. There were plenty of men whom she'd dated across the industry, yet something always felt like a puzzle piece marginally too angular—wrong enough for her to never answer the buzzing phone the next day or accept chocolate boxes in ribbons. Apparently, that alone was a leading cause of her failure.

It started with good-intentioned advice from balding directors on "starting a family," but slowly spiraled out of control with gentle rejections and agents conveniently settling for smaller, more motherly roles. The whole world was telling Rosalyn McCarver, Hollywood's diamond, to leave it while it was still willing to be gracious.

Only she couldn't.

Right now, thousands of miles east, she knew her mother was most likely coughing up blood due to leukemia. A few miles up, and her brother Jack was getting himself rotten drunk for the fifth time this week (it was Friday) and ending up shattering someone's car window. And her father, with his back pains and thin sheets of bills from swiping up boulevards, could hardly sustain anything but three lukewarm meals.

Her parents called her "star" even back in her school days. Perhaps they already knew back then that she was going to become a glittering diamond shining her way through the labyrinth of fame; or perhaps they merely needed hope, a source of light to guide them home every night. No matter the reason, it stuck with her all these years—made her live through brightening the people around her.

Sometimes Rosalyn wondered if stars get tired. If attention meant one had to use one's flesh as fuel to entertain. If endless rotations ever considered the calluses on feet. If beautiful, beautiful light was just the product of collisions between vengeful asteroids and dying bodies.

She laughed silently to herself. "How foolish of you, Rosalyn. To think about that when Mother is withering away without you," she whispered and faced the fact for the first time.

They needed money.

She was running out of money.

This gala, hosted by some stuffy investment firm, was the last chance for her to get a deal out of her decaying stardom before her agents ditched her forever.

She didn't like things being high stakes. Everything came more naturally in bustling sets, where one mistake was easily forgotten and there was too much going around for her to truly matter. But tonight, she realized, she had no choice.

One memory flew through her mind like a streak of light: dirt on her chin, a particularly vibrant carrot in her hand, and her mother standing in front of the kitchen counter. *I want to be a gardener when I grow up, Mama.* A smile with frayed edges and too-thin lines that she should've noticed.

Really? But darling, if you become a gardener, who would help me bake carrot cakes?

Her life was a scale of glamor and grounding, charisma and compliance, flight and floods. In order to obtain eminence, she loosened her grip on family and friendship; now, in search of the hearth she would soon settle in, she had to harmonize the wrecking balls of self-identity and conformity. She knew she needed to keep them always spiraling around each other, carefully poised never to meet and to spark something dangerously extraordinary. Something that would push a star out of orbit, its future vast and enclosed in endless darkness.

The clock on her vanity said quarter to six. The thump in her heart reminded her just what she was capable of—being a star and being a woman; somehow, succeeding at both.

Rosalyn checked her hair one final time, tucked a stray behind her left ear, grabbed a fur coat, and prepared for a night with overly boisterous men.

[three]

Nancy's face was starting to hurt from the smiling. She knew her lips were quivering a bit—starting to not show sixteen of her perfectly porcelain teeth. Perhaps it was the cocktails the servers were handing around, the amount of sugar and liquor sending shivers up her spine. After two glasses, she was already struggling to keep her vision clear and words composed.

On the right side of her, Herbert was conversing cheerily with a colleague. His arm was laced through hers, subtly showing intimacy while not being improper. On normal days, she would've liked the comfort it brought, cherished the ounce of security she felt in a room of leers.

But tonight, everything felt wrong. The things she was saying felt too fake and insincere as she complimented a passing lady's hair accessory. The dress felt too formal and too plain and too everything that made her fidgety. The hand around her wrist felt too hot, the room too small, the music too melancholy.

She couldn't win them over. Not now. Not like this. Desperately and fruitlessly, Nancy planned for an escape.

And then she saw her.

"Hey, gorgeous," the man slurred, eyes roaming greedily.

"Excuse me," Rosalyn replied in the most even voice she could muster and pushed through the crowd. There were couples everywhere; god forbid, she felt like a lacrosse stick painted in neon orange stuck in the middle of a road.

Her age and marital status seemed to stiffen out any interest investors had in her. Three talks later, she was still wandering across the unnaturally white marble floor alone, half-empty glass in one hand and a growing net of worry in the other. The gala seemed to go on without her—the diamond of Hollywood, without any shine at all.

The conversations were dreadful, yet grabbing every chance she was presented with, Rosalyn started to greet another one of the potential investors.

And then she saw her.

She was wearing one of those sheath dresses only seen in high-budget movies—a moving silhouette of Persian blue with golden earrings, necklace, and heels. Nancy could almost recall her name, but awe took everything away but the sight of her walking toward them.

She looked straight from a commercial with her lilac patterned gown; the cinched-in waist and dramatic flair at the bottom twirled a little every time she bobbed from side to side. Rosalyn restrained her smile as their gazes met and her round eyes widened.

Nancy Periweather knew too much about pain to realize the joy consuming her.

Rosalyn McCarver knew too little about unplanned desire to notice her burning skin.

When Boer initially discovered his close-to-exact model of an atom, he knew with thousands of years' worth of knowledge behind him that it was destined to metamorphose in and out of molecules—blink in and out of existence. So he named this eternal process of collision something pretty to balance out the explosions: bonding.

The government had something different in mind. Thirteen years later, countless families would cheer in front of their televisions, conveniently forgetting the war raging eons east, as a man's white boots collided with the dusty skin of the moon. They would watch in awe as he sprung up and leaped forward, proving the pinnacle of humankind.

But Nancy and Rosalyn didn't know this—nor did they know about the upcoming rendezvous in highway hotel rooms, the new brand deals following new hues of smoking vermillion eyeshadow, the familiar suburban home now littered with pink leather boots alongside brown. Not enough was known about collisions; certainly not enough to pinpoint it at this moment, recognize anything but the eruption of flapping flames in their chests.

So when they did relive that day through honeyed dinnertime stories with grandchildren, they'd only mention the simplest things: the sweet aftertaste of martini, the overlapping shadows of heels across gold-etched mirrors, and the deceptive sensation that in between two trifling seconds, the clock's hands had forgotten to move.

Biscuits & Rain

"Vincent Avenue, Number 29."

Clara mumbled the address as a confirmation, hands on warm brass doorknobs and nostrils suddenly filled with the buttery scent of bread; her stomach gurgled immediately, the uneaten lunch making its presence known. It had been three weeks since she moved to New York City, so she followed Google Maps after seven hours of endless Excel sheets to . . .

"Clara?"

She looked up and almost stumbled over. "Aiden?"

And all thoughts were lost as she saw *him* standing behind the counter, a dark contrast to the checkered tablecloths and pale yellow walls. The angle of the lift of his eyebrows and the mole on the tip of his right earlobe were all exactly the same, yet she felt sweat forming on the top of her forehead.

"You moved?" he asked, voice slightly too loud.

Shoulders tightening to force her gaze up, Clara replied, "Why? Best job opportunity and tons of friends here, so of course! I moved, so what?" *Damnit, you're saying too much, idiot.* She kept herself from mentioning how this was the only job offer she got after grad school.

They stared at each other for several seconds. Her memory sparked up at the familiar hue of ocean blue, on grass fields in the middle of July and spiked sodas and three thousand hours of . . .

"Uh, good for you, then." He shifted, dropping the eye contact and wrinkling his nose. "Do you want anything?"

Shoot. She'd almost forgotten this was a bakery. Grabbing the nearest item she could find, she squeezed her cheeks into something that resembled a smile, albeit a painful one. "Sure, I'll get these . . ." What is that? " . . . biscuits."

He glanced at her fingers that were now clutching the package like an overprotective claw machine. "I didn't know you liked biscuits."

"Seems like you don't know me well at all, then." She met his eyes and expected to see hurt or sorrow or anger or anything that indicated emotion.

Instead, Aiden just furrowed his brows a little, then chuckled.

"Still as aggressive as ever. Want these packed up?"

"Yes, please."

"That'll be three dollars, plus fifty cents for the bag."

"Fifty. For a bag. You got to be kidding me." Clara bit her tongue and wondered why he was still demanding money from her. Three months erased many, many things, but apparently, not this.

He gave her a classic 45-degree smile. "We're discouraging plastic waste, I'm afraid. State orders." He emphasized the word state.

Heat bubbled beneath her face like an insidious wave, and an anger she remembered as her name roared in her mind. "Of course, I know about the state orders," she snapped. "Three-fifty then."

Three bills and one coin. An electric shock flew up to her arm as their fingers touched briefly and she almost stepped back involuntarily.

He handed her the bag, and she found her fingers lingering near the edge he folded seconds ago. "Well, I'll be on my way then," she let out.

Taking one last look at the golden, dimmed lights and speckled floor (and Aiden's pink blush matching his apron), Clara turned to leave . . .

. . . And was greeted by a blinding sliver of lightning right outside the door, followed by the sound of rain on stone pavements.

Today. It had to be today that she forgot to bring an umbrella. She mouthed a few inventive curses, then slowly turned back toward Aiden.

Another staring contest of blue against brown, making her head a little dizzy.

"So . . ." she started.

"So . . ."

"I guess we should catch up," she stated, trying to soften her voice so it wouldn't quiver.

He shrugged. "Sure."

Hating how relaxed he sounded, she strode up to the counter again and smiled.

"How're things going with Liliana?"

Silence for a few seconds, the darkened sky reflecting onto glass jars behind the counter like a circlet of resurfacing, unpleasant memories.

The slight wrinkle of his brows warmed the tips of her clammy fingers.

"Clara . . ."

"Is she making you happy like she used to?" Clara continued, her smile widening.

Aiden widened his eyes and made a small, unrecognizable sound that resembled a squirm. "It was a mistake, Clara, please . . ."

"A damn convenient mistake."

Her heart was thudding, feeling the old burst of excitement from making him mad; she loved how they fought, in rain and malls, between classes and after dinner, the taste of salty tears combined with the warmth of his hug. The rain sounds were getting louder, almost covering his voice.

"I've told you that night and I'm telling you again, but you never listen to me, you—"

"Don't you dare blame it on me, Aiden Malcolm Webster—"

"How the hell am I blaming it on you? I never—"

"Damn right, you never cared about our relationship or else that night would've never happened—"

"You know she was drunk, Clara, she was my friend. I can't—"

"And I was your girlfriend, for fuc—"

"It was a goddamn car ride, you have no proof—"

"Why did you end up with a stupid smile on your face at the end, then—"

"People are allowed to smile, Jesus—"

"You never smiled like that around me, you were never happy with me—"

"I was always happy with you. For God's sake, I loved you every single second—"

"Then get back together with me, you bastard!"

Clara realized what she said right after the words came out, and she clamped her mouth to prevent any further sound from forming. No, she did not. She did not just admit her desire of getting back together with her ex. In front of her ex. Right in the middle of a goddamn downpour.

Moving her feet slightly, she tried her very best to straighten her face and look unfazed. But all failed when something started glittering in Aiden's eyes. Something that made her heart pause for a moment in utter embarrassment.

Something like . . . pity?

Lightning crackled behind her, illuminating the outline of his curls. For a moment, he looked like an angel exiled from heaven, his profile's sharp contours reminiscent of marble statues and folklore. Too beautiful, always kind, never hers.

"Come on, Clara," he started, voice surprisingly gentle compared to his harsh tone just seconds before. "You know that—"

"Of course, I know," she cut him off, not wanting to hear the rejection out loud. "I, um, said that out of, um, anger. It doesn't mean anything, don't worry."

She swallowed, dry throat aching a little. But she knew that it hurt more to open herself up, flesh adorned with flowers and ready to be slaughtered.

As the thunder finally screamed into the sky, Clara felt her heart shatter into little Liliana-shaped pieces, falling onto the ground in the form of the girl Aiden loved most.

"All right, just making sure," he said.

"Yeah," she replied, attempting not to meet his gaze by focusing on the particular shape of her boot's tip.

The rain showed no sign of stopping with continuous rumbles, adding a thick blanket of gray mist onto the store's only window. She started to try to extend her toes within her boots, unsure of what to say next.

"Um, if you wanna eat anything, just take it," Aiden broke the silence. "The bread isn't gonna get sold anyway in this weather."

"I'm good," Clara said instinctively, and then saw the glazed donuts topped with candy sprinkles, cleanly sliced baguettes sparkling with garlic sauce, freshly baked oatmeal cookies with the raisins practically singing with saccharine satisfaction.

"Maybe just one," she finished meekly.

And so that was how the two ended up sitting side by side on the floor, stuffing their faces with more food than they could count. Sometime in the middle of an awkward conversation about dentists, he asked, "You didn't take any biscuits?"

"Oh." Shoot. "Uh, I'm saving it for later."

"All right."

Then a thought suddenly popped up in her mind. "So, are you together with Liliana or not?"

"No, we're just friends," he answered quickly, then added in a more careful tone, "I'm seeing someone else though."

"What's her name?" Somehow that was important. So that Clara could visualize her and compare the two of them, side by side.

"Abigail."

Abigail, she imagined, would be a petite redhead with soft hands and a bohemian sense of fashion. Abigail would love cooking foreign dishes and prefer dogs to cats and go on hikes in her spare time. Abigail would be the complete opposite of brunette, old-fashioned, and organized Clara, but Aiden would love Abagail more all the same.

"Abigail," she repeated, the sound like a wisp of smoke on her lips, "Her name sounds dazzling."

"She is," he said and flashed the largest, most genuine smile she had ever seen.

Oh well; maybe Abigail really is something.

"What about you?" he asked, pulling her thoughts back, "You dating anyone?"

"No, I just moved and all." She never went back on the market after they broke up, rationality losing to the ache for golden, curling hair across rooms and the bursts of repulsion every time she tried to hold someone intimately.

"Of course, that was a dumb question."

Silence, only more comfortable this time.

They heard the rain getting smaller and smaller until the faint sounds of tapping on doors disappeared altogether. The window's blurry view slowly changed from dark gray to a lighter blue.

It had ended.

Clara stood up first, smoothing out the wrinkles of fabric near her thighs and watching Aiden bounce to his feet the next second. He returned to his place behind the counter, apron slightly skewed, and she inched closer to the door, although still facing him.

"I think I should go," she said quietly, voice slightly raspy although her cheeks had cooled and her hands steady.

"Great, uh, it was nice to see you," he replied, looking sheepish.

"It was nice to see you too," she said and found that she actually meant it. After months of trying to forget him, this small, unexpected meeting somehow made more progress. In some way, seeing his solid frame had shattered the rosy images of him that once spiraled her mind and prevented omission; sensing his happiness ignited her desire for the same.

"Uh, do you want more biscuits? I hate to see you leave after hours with just a small bag," he asked, words slow and carrying an upward lilt.

She took a deep breath and stood a little taller. The warm afterglow framed the two of them right across their cheekbones, as if they just escaped from an 1800's oil painting of picnic pastries and petrichor and soft, unrequited pining for brooding men.

"No, I think I'm good," Clara answered. She thought of ending it there, but decided to continue with a subtle grin, "I don't like biscuits that well."

And with that, she left the store without a second glance at Aiden's slightly open mouth, fingers already sticky with the biscuits' oil leaking through the bag, the damp air and fresh scent of grass clinging around her.

Her lungs demanded something more.

Taking one scan at the splatter of puddles around her and children playing with water guns in every shade, she started to run the fastest she could, the speed washing out worries about her hair smudging her lipstick or how the muddy water gripped onto her newly bought coat.

As the sun shook hands with the moon, the whole sky stared at a small, insignificant figure tromping her way down the street, until she slowly disappeared off of the horizon.

Criminal #1240

The room was white. A spotless kind—they obviously renovated it after the Riot, and they did it well. Two white plastic chairs surrounded a white table, a white door behind one and a white box behind the other. The white tiled floors sent shivers up my bare feet.

On one of the white chairs sat a white man with white hair and a white suit. His dark blue eyes and my orange robe were the only colorful things I saw. He did not speak when I entered, yet his gaze followed me as I moved.

I could barely feel my legs when I finally sunk into my chair, its sharp angles pointing into my flesh slightly. I could hear the voices in the back of my mind coaxing me to stand up, to run away, to get as far as I could from the white room and the man who was now tying a band around my wrist. It connected to the white box. Perhaps the white box was filled with poison that would kill me slowly, one cell at a time. Perhaps it was a power engine, and I was merely a robot who lived off the powder of ancient corpses. Perhaps the white box would take away my blood, making me faint so they could do whatever they wanted with me.

Run, Leia, run, they whispered, words tumbling over one another. *Cut off the band. Upturn the table. Claw at his throat. Run.*

I stayed put.

The man started speaking only after he swiftly tapped on the white box twice. "Officer Gardner." His voice was deep and smooth, like wine from the 2010s that aged finely in a manor's cellar.

"Pleasure to meet you," I heard my voice reply. When did I decide to speak? "Leia Solis."

He started writing on his clipboard and didn't bother to reply. I could faintly see the bold text on the top of the page.

"Suspect #1240."

$1 + 2 + 4 = 7$, my mind automatically thought. A prime number. No divisibility rules: you had to divide it out by hand. Unpredictable and annoying yet solved countless seemingly complex equations.

Stop thinking about math, the voices snapped. *That never awarded you anything remotely positive.*

So, I thought about the seven days of the week instead. Or the seven colors of the rainbow. Anything to prevent me from looking at Officer Gardner and my name below the word "suspect."

"Ms. Solis, this conversation will involve the lie detector. We're required to notify you in advance. Do you consent?" Officer Gardner asked, his eyes still on the clipboard.

The voices started hissing, their sounds drowning out my lucid thoughts; for a moment, all I could hear were a thousand little phrases circling around my head like summer mosquitos, too distant to catch and too proximal to ignore.

I heard myself say, "And what if I don't, Officer Gardner?" They died down, triumphant.

The officer finally looked up at me. I realized his eyes had a golden edge to them. "Ms. Solis," he repeated, pausing in between every syllable, "do you consent?"

I desperately tried to cling on, to remain in the room, to control my lips before another word slipped out. I focused on the white box. Perhaps that was the lie detector. Or perhaps it was still a weapon used to contort the edges of my features and haunt the corridors of my mind—to control me and kill me, slowly.

Perhaps it was both.

I bit my lip, a little too hard. Salt stung my mouth. "I consent, sir," I replied, focusing on smoothing out every sibilant sound as I realized I finally said something I wanted.

"All right. Let's start, then." He nibbled at the tip of his pen when he was thinking. Just like Samantha.

Oh, Samantha. My heart ached, and suddenly in front of me stood my willowy sister, her hands outstretched, an adventure already unfolding with the tips of our fingers intertwined. *Don't be a bore, Leia. We can have fun.* I reached out instinctively, yet the moment I moved, blood sprouted in the middle of her chest, its shadow staining her white dress and covering her body bit by bit, until all I could see was red.

I must have flinched, because Officer Gardner glanced toward me. "Age?"

"Twenty-eight." My throat was turning to flakes. When was the last time they gave me water?

"Father's name?"

Through my clouded memories, I searched for clues of his existence. A cigar in worn hands and my desperate urge to eat it (eat anything) were all I could remember. "Thomas Solis," I answered, the rhythm of his name twisting the tip of my tongue.

"Mother's name?"

"Arelia Solis."

"Good," Officer Gardner murmured. "No lies yet."

I wanted to punch him. I wanted to grab his hair and tell him he knew nothing—nothing about me or my past or whether I was lying. I wanted to tear him up into little pieces and tell him beautiful, almost truthful lies until he died.

Do it. Do it. Do it.

"Any siblings?" he continued.

My throat clogged for a moment, currents of sound fighting against boulders of grief. "Samantha Solis. She was supposed to turn twenty-three two months ago."

The pen paused slightly, then kept on going. If I just focused on the pen, it was almost like Officer Gardner didn't exist, and all that was in the room was a magical, moving pen and me.

Sounded like that ancient novel *Harry Potter*. I remembered it being banned at my school yet still making appearances on confiscated notes and recess chants.

"Ms. Solis, what were you doing at 8 p.m. on January 23?"

Of course. Now the actual interrogation began. I tried to recall that night, yet nothing seemed to spark in my dull, gray field of thoughts without the voices' presence. It was late, which meant I probably stayed at home; around a week ago, which meant I was painting the kitchen.

The voices teased me. They wanted me to answer something false, something so clearly untrue that even Officer Gardner could tell. *Have a little fun with him, Leia.*

Not when my life was on the line.

When has it been safe, darling? When were you ever safe?

My head hurting, I gritted my teeth and told as many truths as I could. "I was in the process of redecorating my kitchen, sir. I was probably painting a wall or reordering my cookware."

I tried to speak as vaguely as possible, because letting Officer Gardner know about the fact that I was painting everything in my house black would not help defend my innocence. I desperately needed to drown out the voices, and living in a dark pit seemed to scare them away.

On the contrary, being in a white room like this made them extra excited.

"Ms. Solis, what did you do that day?" he pressed on, pen not stopping. I assumed I passed the lie detector test.

"Oh, the usual, sir. I woke up at six forty-five to go to work, since I usually use the metro." How long was the line? "I arrived at the office at eight o'clock sharp, and stayed there until five thirty." Or was it five forty-five? Did I finish the report on time? "I ate lunch inside my building. Then, I rode the metro back and arrived home at six thirty. I ordered my dinner and started redecorating my room until around ten, and then I got ready for bed."

I left out the details, of course. How I barely got to the metro station before the seven-o-five ride took off, my eyes puffy from the night before. How the printing machine in the office stopped working and the two girls beside my station—Bertha Collins and Michelle Yeung, I think—started whispering about how things only started to break down after "the lunatic" arrived. How there was a bug in my lunchbox. How I didn't eat the dinner I ordered after the scale revealed two increased pounds. How after the "decorations" there were tears and broken vases and sharp objects that drew crimson.

But not on others. Never on others. Crimson only on my own skin.

The officer stopped writing. I wondered if I left out too much and he would be angry. Perhaps he would slap my face—reminiscent of my first boyfriend, the stale odor of alcohol permeating the room and hands landing across my face. Or perhaps he would turn into the man I saw on the sidewalk right before I got my first job, fingers pressing down on my wrists and leaving dark bruises.

Slap him. Fight him. Kill him before he kills you, the voices whispered urgently. My wrist froze, preparing to seize a strong, searching hand.

Yet he started to speak.

"Ms. Solis, would you mind playing a game?" Officer Gardner asked casually, as if we weren't in the police station in a country with record-strict laws, especially after the Riot and the whispers of resistance (and blood) that once flooded the streets. As if we were just two friends chatting about work, with no consequences and half-hidden lies behind every word.

I didn't respond. I didn't know how to. Was this a trick question? Would he use this against me in some way? *They're always trick questions.*

Officer Gardner continued, as if through my silence I somehow agreed. "Tell me two truths and one lie, Ms. Solis."

Perhaps this was a game, or some mind trick. I wanted to obey the voices, to hurl over the desk, to see the look of shock in Officer Gardner's blue-and-gold eyes before I forced them shut forever; burst open the box to discover all the books my mother muttered about in her sleep yet never dared utter out loud.

My body felt so, so tired.

"My sister died in the Riot. She got shot in the middle of carrying a wounded police officer back to safety." My voice came out smaller than I expected it to be, yet it pushed through the chilly air and slammed into his face all the same.

Officer Gardner started writing.

"I was on medication for anxiety, yet the doctor refused to give me more because he was scared of an overdose." My brain processed my words after they had been spoken, and I couldn't quite believe the specificity and intimacy, yet a familiar ache in my heart told me otherwise.

Two years of dead parents and dead sisters and dead relatives and dead friendships and dead everything except for slowing heartbeats—waking me up in the middle of the night like reminders of transience.

Lie an obvious lie. Lie something that will make him remember you.

As if grabbing on the last straw before quicksand consumed me whole, I gave in.

"I killed Bertha Collins."

Officer Gardner did not stop writing for a few seconds. I stared at the white box and wondered if it knew all my secrets. The deepest ones. Even the time where I changed an answer when I saw a note being passed in front of me, which gave me a test score just high enough to get in my top university.

"Interesting, Ms. Solis." His voice was smooth, too smooth. "Would you like to know my guess? Or rather, the answer since I have the lie detector's results."

I nodded, a slight dip of my chin.

I saw the movement of his lips before I heard his words. "The lie is the medication, isn't it?"

My mind went blank with irritation. I did, in fact, get rejected by the doctor, and I did have anxiety. The terrible kind. The kind that made you tear out your hair and scrub the floor until blisters form on your hands and drink so many glasses of iced americano you barely get an hour of sleep every night. *The kind that caused your failure.* "You must be mistaken, Officer Gardner. Because that is true," I answered carefully, searching for any signs of mischief—surely the lie detector would not be so inaccurate.

There was no sign.

"Why do you think that is true, Ms. Solis?" Officer Gardner asked softly.

"Because it happened to me, sir." What was he trying to say?

"Yes, but the lie detector clearly showed that was a lie, Ms. Solis. Are you trusting your flawed brain over a machine refined over a century with 100 percent accuracy?" he pushed.

"But—"

"Ms. Solis, what type of medication were you on?"

I concentrated on my thoughts—and couldn't remember. I remember the doctor's hand, and I remember the doctor's face, and I remember the small blue box he gave me. Yet I couldn't remember the small black letters, printed on the front with a seal, its texture a little rougher than the other parts of the box.

I rummaged around my memory, bit by bit. *Come on, Leia. Be useful for once.* Yet, I just couldn't recall anything.

"Was it fentanyl, perhaps?" Officer Gardner suggested.

Maybe it did start with an *F*. "I think so, sir."

He looked at me, a slight dent forming in between his brows. "Ms. Solis, I'm very sure that you're aware fentanyl is a highly dangerous and addictive drug."

I shook my head. I never craved my medicine, even though the anxiety got worse after the doctor stopped giving them to me. "Then I think you said the wrong medication, sir."

"Oh," Officer Gardner replied. "But you see, the lie detector shows your previous statements to be true."

I forgot how to breathe.

Almost hysterically, I tear through my recollections of the days at the hospital, trying to cling on to words, letters, phrases. Anything other than fentanyl. Yet somehow, when I looked back at the blue box, I see the word FENTANYL printed on the package in a small, black font, its texture a little rougher than the other parts of the box.

What was real? What was not?

I looked at other memories. Fentanyl started appearing in them too. I could even hear my doctor say the word, his voice clipped as always.

"Ms. Solis," Officer Gardner whispered, "were you taking drugs like fentanyl recently?"

Fentanyl. Fentanyl. Fentanyl.

Stop it.

The room was spinning. Was the box robin-egg blue? Or was it a pale pink?

"Yes," I heard my voice say. I couldn't move my lips or fingers. It was like having sleep paralysis: you see the turquoise box expanding and swallowing the room bit by bit but can't do a thing as you get engulfed in shades of too-vivid green.

"Thank you for your honesty, Ms. Solis. Now, it seems that your statement about your sister was true for the most part. Yet you made up the part about the police officer, didn't you?"

As desperately and as futilely as last time, I tried to remember. Samantha, running around on the grass. Samantha, twirling around in the small alley in between our house and the communal bathroom. Samantha, dragging a man to the side of the road after school, her hands covered with his blood.

"I understand that you're trying to protect your sister, Ms. Solis," Officer Gardner continued. "However, you don't need to hide anything from us. She was saving a Rioter, wasn't she?"

The face of the man was blurry in my mind. I never looked at him, not before the shot and the bullet that seemed so slow and the red stain that immediately started spreading, right over Samantha's heart.

"Did your sister save a Rioter, Ms. Solis?"

Samantha, my angel. Samantha, my reason to live. Samantha, who died in my arms five minutes later—just weeks after her fourteenth birthday, who never saw the university I promised to take her to the next day. *Samantha, who died because of you and entered the ground believing you left her.*

"Ms. Solis?"

"I don't know!" I screamed, suddenly having the urge to throw my head into the white, not-so-white-table and watch it become a pure, clean ruby. "I don't remember! I don't know!"

The faceless man ran off as I howled Samantha's name, right next to a group of Rioters with guns and laser cutters. What was on his face? A scar?

Why would a police officer have a scar?

Yet I remember he wore a uniform. Or was it merely a construction worker's attire?

"Yes, yes, yes." Tears blurred my vision, as Officer Gardner blurred into the background until everything in the room was one big object, roaming above me.

"And finally," Officer Gardner said, voice low. He glanced at me. His eyes were gold now. "You killed Bertha Collins."

I did not know Bertha Collins. But then, maybe I did. Everything in my mind was jumbled, torn, scraps of half-truths and half-lies. As I thought about it, maybe my kitchen wall was covered in blood. Bertha Collins's or mine, I didn't know.

But the lie detector did. The lie detector knew the truths and the lies all along. Even though everything about me was in the middle.

"Yes, I did, Officer Gardner."

The voices had erupted. They crashed through my skull, filling the room with smoke and fire, covering the white wooden chairs with ashes and debris. I saw myself jumping up and bolting toward the door, only to be dragged back to the seat by the firm iron chains around my wrist.

"Leia Solis, there is ample evidence to prove your murder of Bertha Collins at 8 p.m. on January 23. Please stay in the room while the guards arrive."

I laughed. He was probably right. I probably did kill Bertha Collins. The marble floor's patterns were spinning, turning, evolving into the faces of my doctor and the Rioter and Samantha and Officer Gardner and Bertha Collins. They rose up around me, voices so familiar, chanting a phrase over and over again until I found myself joining them.

"Criminal #1240. Criminal #1240. Criminal #1240."

Sacrifice

August 31st, 1888

"Miss."

She looked up, hands trembling slightly because of the sudden sound, and peered at the stranger through the early fog of London mixed with the aftermath of cheap alcohol.

Dressed in a black light waistcoat and trousers, he looked proper enough, at least compared to the "gentlemen" who came and went on this street. Only his gray, sharp eyes were moving, scanning her too-frail body, and she could almost hear his thoughts.

Pretty if not too heavy on the makeup, experienced, and a year left at best in her career.

Batting the rising nausea from her stomach away quickly (not quickly enough), she straightened her skirt, even though she knew it was battered around the edges and one spot even had a stain. Perhaps he wouldn't notice. Men who came and went in this area weren't careful like that—didn't needed to be, with their mud-stained bills and crooked teeth.

"Can I help you, sir?" she asked, plastering her voice with honey and spiced cinnamon. It always seemed to work, yet the man's expression didn't as much as flinch for a second.

"Unfortunately, I am quite lost, miss," he said, with a hint of nervous laughter, and she noted the vowels he rushed over. Scottish. "I have a scheduled meeting with an old friend at number 29, Hanbury Street, and I checked the map multiple times, but I still haven't got a single clue where that is."

Now it was her turn to eye him from head to toe. He did have a traveler's aura around him, with a scratchy chin, dark circles under his eyes, and dirt on his clearly expensive boots.

Her mind skimmed through the evidence and searched for the shadows of suspicion. No signs of alcohol or opium use. Most likely from the middle-to-upper class. Foreigner to London.

Relatively safe.

Perhaps even a potential customer, if he was staying for longer.

"Well," she answered, attempting to fix loose curls falling from her bun, "I'm quite familiar with this area of London, sir, and if you'll allow me, I can surely show you the way."

He broke into a relieved smile. "That would be much appreciated, miss."

She felt her eyes narrow at the "miss," knowing very well that the clear wrinkles framing her face indicated nothing shorter than four decades of turmoil, but she led the way down the street, him following a few paces behind.

He politely made conversation along the way, and she politely responded, trying to ignore the warm summer wind against her cheeks. *It'll turn chilly soon, and you'll be cursing the weather when the lodging house becomes Antarctica before its discovery*, she chided herself, then realized she might not even have the money to return to the lodging house this winter.

Buggers.

Forcefully tugging her thoughts back, she stopped in front of a brownstone building. "And here you have it, sir: number 29, Hanbury Street."

He surveyed it with interest for a few moments, then turned back to her. "That was awfully kind of you to show me all the way here, Miss . . ." He looked at her expectantly.

"Nichols," she stuttered.

Her mother, fingers pressing into her cheeks, sunlight iridescent behind the jam jars.

When she pulled her attention back, her nails already formed ten crescent-shaped prints at the end of her tightly intertwined wrists.

The street was free of its usual sounds of impatient proletarians and empty save for a young woman walking by on the opposite side of the road. A crow fluttered somewhere above her head.

"Miss Nichols," he continued. "Now I owe you a great deal, and I'm not sure how to repay it."

"Oh, no worries, sir," she laughed. How completely naive and natural of him to believe she could be helped. "It was a pleasure talking with you. I'll be on my way then, and you have a great visit with your friend."

She turned to go, mind already crowded with the long, insidious day ahead of her without customers and therefore money and therefore any ounce of relative weight on this planet.

A hand snatched her arm.

She turned, surprised, to see herself face-to-face with the stranger. His eyes, still sharp and gray, carried a new kind of light. One she had never seen before.

"I cannot let you go without repaying you, I'm afraid," he whispered.

And at that moment she realized with horror that he spoke perfect London English without even a hint of Scottish accent.

"I—"

"Now, keep quiet, Miss Nichols." Fingernails digging into her skin. "I know just the favor for you."

A metallic glint in the soft sunlight. Sharp edges. Everything around her turned liquid, and she suddenly found herself falling, falling, into the dark pits of her memories.

Five years old and in the tiny yet warm kitchen of her childhood house, sitting on a wooden stool, watching her mother cook dinner in a colossal iron pot.

"Mama, why can't I go out and play like Fountain?" she whined, peering out the window to see her older brother running down the street with his buddies, chasing after a mangy cat with blotchy fur and sepia-colored whiskers.

"Honey, we have had this conversation dozens of times," her mother answered, voice carrying a hoarse edge around pauses and hand still stirring the soup. "Boys like your brother are adventurous by nature. Now, you, Mary, you are a lady, and ladies must stay within the house, where they thrive. You're Mama's little helper; right, young lady?"

The word "lady" suddenly made the iron pot gleam a little more. She bobbed her head three times, hoping her mother could see the light reflected in her eyes. "Of course, Mama!"

She was ten and tried to hide under her patched-up blanket as her father's distinguishable footsteps clamped on the front doorstep irregularly, an empty glass bottle in one hand and some ripped-up papers in the other.

Her mother's soft voice, clearly angry. "Edward, it's past midnight."

"Don't talk to me like that, woman."

A gasp. "And suddenly unemployed too? What are we going to do now? You have three children, Edward, and yet you . . ."

She anticipated the slap before she heard it—sometimes, she wondered if pain was like lightning and thunder, its presence already so clearly indicated beforehand yet always surprisingly loud.

"Stop. Being. Disrespectful." Words hissed through his mouth like poison.

She covered herself a little more, as if curling into a fetal shape would return her to two inches and a few feathers' worth of gravitational pull.

"You can't possibly . . ." her mother attempted to continue.

The sound of glass shattering. She could smell the leftover alcohol that started to stain her blanket, hear her mother's barely concealed screams, feel her brothers twitch silently beside her.

The next morning, she woke up early to clean up the blood.

"Mother, why can't you two split or . . . divorce?"

Her mother glanced up sharply from her cutting, eyebrows unusually flattened. "I don't know what your teachers are telling you, Mary, but that's utterly inappropriate."

"But—" she desperately tried to argue her hopeless case.

"Don't ever bring it up again."

Her first time in silk, hands on the Bible, staring into the eyes of a stranger.

"I take thee to be my husband, to have and to hold from this day forward, for better or for worse, for richer, for poorer, in sickness and in health, to love and to cherish; and I promise to be faithful to you until death parts us."

The thrum in her vein matched the joyous sound of a passing ensemble outside.

"Mama, why can't I go outside to play like Teddy?"

She looked lovingly at her daughter, hands still powdery from kneading the dough. "You're a lady, Isabella, and ladies must stay within the house, where they thrive. Now, you're Mama's little helper, right?"

Isabella looked up, and the light within her daughter's eyes reminded her of long-abandoned iron pots. "Of course, Mama," she chimed.

The front door opened and her husband shouted, "Ladies!" and her daughter ran from her embrace to meet him, and it was everything she had dreamed of back in the liquor-stained bedsheets of her childhood.

Until it wasn't.

"I. Never. Wear. This. Type. Of. Perfume." Words whispered through her mouth as the spicy scent around her husband engulfed her.

"Mary." His voice was low and fuzzy around the edges, a tell-tale sign before a loud slap on the table or a slam of the birchwood doors. "Don't you bloody dare tell me what to do."

"Of course, I dare to. I am your perfect wife and your children's perfect mother, yet you decided to repay me with infidelity like the piece of—"

A sharp, instantaneous spike of pain. It was only after a few seconds, when she peered at the darkened window behind her, that she realized her face was red and swollen.

He stood before her, calm and collected, so different yet so similar to her father. A glance upon her over his nose, and he left their bedroom.

Something hardened inside her heart, heavy like iron. This time, she would not fade away.

At her mother's funeral, she didn't cry. Not one bit.

It was only until she arrived at her room in the lodging house that she allowed herself to break down, to remember the slight lowering of lids onto her mother's dull eyes as she said, "Mother, we divorced today."

After being called a lady for the first thirty years of her life, she was left with a suitcase, two scar-ridden hands, and the absence of sunlight in a fifty-square-foot room.

The first time, she almost threw up when he looked at her with those muddy eyes, telling her to scream his name.

Slowly, she got used to it, to the smell of smoke in the alleys and men who whistled at her every time she passed them. She learned to apply rouge and powder, learned to wink at and flirt with potential customers, learned to stock large amounts of lemon and vinegar in her closet.

But she still lowered her head with bile forming behind her throat whenever a stranger asked her about her job, and between consciousness and sleep she still couldn't stop repeating the whispers of housewives as she walked by every night.

"Prostitute. Slut. Unclean. Better off dead."

Carolina took her out for a drink on the second year and showed her how to flirt with bartenders so they could get free drinks, and she taught her how to buy cheap alcohol or the best ratio of rum to vodka.

She fell in love with it.

And so she drank and drank and drank.

She drank when her children pretended not to recognize her when she saw them across the street. She drank when her customers got a little too rough and gave her cuts or bruises all over her body. She drank when she heard her ex-husband married the mistress and everyone said they couldn't be more compatible together.

She drank even after her money stack became paper-thin and dear Carolina was found dead one morning, a half-empty beer bottle in one hand.

Because how could she remain awake when the cold, biting air of London gave nothing to her but frostbite after a long walk from her post followed by iron-like shackles of averted gazes?

She refocused. The Scottish-but-not-Scottish man in front of her, a sharp object tilted lightly at her throat, the thick English fog draping around her like the silk dress she could never wear again.

His eyes were almost lazy, scanning across her face slowly, a hint of a smile at his lips blooming like nightshade.

"Any last words, Miss Nichols?" His tone was soft, smooth, polite, lethal.

She almost laughed. Who would care about her last words? Just another girl on the street, living off of her flesh that was quickly becoming rottenly undesirable.

And at that moment, she realized, with the alcohol finally cleansed from her body, that she wanted to smell the baker's fresh bread one more time, argue with the lodging house's keeper about delaying her rent one more night, give her daughter's beautiful townhouse one more peek as she walked by.

Finally, she wanted desperately to live, but she could feel the warm liquid flowing down her throat and clouding her vision.

"Why . . ." she choked out.

Clear laughter, fading out.

Just one more second . . .

Just one more . . .

Just one . . .

Just . . .

She lost consciousness.

And so Mary Ann Nichols would never see the police's horror when they discovered her severed body, her son's reddened eyes, the girls in her lodging house who began to walk with their head tall, and the newspapers with titles like "WHO IS TO BLAME FOR HER MURDER: THE KNIFE OR THE CIRCUMSTANCES?"

She would never know her role in a newly awakened movement that would shake the world, never live in this society she helped create.

Because she was, like all the others, just another beautiful, ordinary, broken girl on the street.

Counseling Core

If the students of St. Barbara High were to predict where Florence Chandler would be during Tuesday lunch, none would say the counselor's office. In fact, the answer would vary as you wandered through the spotless cafeteria, interrogating table after table, but nothing would even come close.

"In the library, I presume," muttered Bridgette Irvin, hands protectively wrapped around her black mug. "She could've at least told me since I bought her coffee."

"Doing the physics project?" Lee O'Brien guessed with a genuine tone, a National Honor Society sticker on his opened computer. "Obviously I finished it, but I heard it's quite a challenge for many, so I won't be surprised if she's working on it now."

"Club meeting," answered Raya McKay, giving a swift side-eyed glance to her friends nearby. "She's the ultimate overachiever, you know? Of course, she would have ten thousand clubs."

Nate Wong and his table laughed at the question. "Flirting with the teachers. Girl gotta get her A, respect!" he stage whispered, earning even more chuckles.

"I wouldn't know," Emma Greenwood snapped, and walked off to buy an ice cream, her bracelets tinkling.

But, of course, they were all wrong (except maybe Emma). Because the girl in question was opening the office door of Mrs. Vess, the junior counselor, at precisely 1:05 P.M. The sharp sound of her boots joined the ringing of the Christmas bells on the door handle; she herself was utterly silent.

"Ms. Chandler!" Mrs. Vess's boisterous voice announced. "I'm very, very glad to see you!"

"Thank you, Mrs. Vess," Florence answered, her brows lifting slightly.

"Please, make yourself at home," the counselor said, even though Florence was already sitting down on a cobalt-blue armchair, her face carefully hidden with side bangs.

After both had settled in, Mrs. Vess leaned forward eagerly. "So, it's a rare sight seeing you in my office, Florence."

"Yes, Mrs. Vess."

"And I suppose"—a pause—"you know why you're here today."

"Yes, Mrs. Vess."

The woman leaned in further, her eyes glowing with yellow-hued light. "Before we get started, I just want to say that I'm extremely, extremely sorry for—"

"Thank you, Mrs. Vess," Florence cut her off as she was taking a breath. "I appreciate you being here for me."

"Of course, dear. Now tell me, what's been going on lately for you?"

The counselor asked the question without a rise in tone, yet Florence flinched slightly, her eyes still fixed on a faraway point somewhere on the room's brightly painted windows.

"Nothing much, Mrs. Vess. The AP courses are as always, and choir is hurting my throat a little, but I'm doing good as usual," she responded after a moment.

Mrs. Vess's smile wavered for a moment as the first ray of afternoon sunlight slid into the office. "Florence, darling," she pushed, "you know you can tell me anything, right?"

Florence smiled non-committedly. "Of course, it's just my life isn't very eventful, as you know."

She took a glance at the picture wall on her left. It was filled with paintings from the elementary students: oil pastels and charcoals and acrylics. In the center was a Sharpie drawing with two stick figures (one with a bowtie), a dog-like animal, and sloppy letters that spelled out "FERN VESS."

Mrs. Vess took this as a cue and leaned in further, which successfully grabbed Florence's attention. "So, who's the lucky guy?" she asked conspiratorially.

Florence shifted, her brows scrunching a little. "I'm sorry, what?"

"Oh, you don't fool me one bit, honeypie," the counselor replied, her hands now tapping on the table merrily. "I know what caused that breakdown." She lowered her voice dramatically. "It's lovesickness, isn't it?"

"Um, Mrs. Vess—"

"Darling, don't lie to me. You can tell me anything, right?"

"I don't understand what you're implying, ma'am," Florence said. She was leaning back in her armchair, as if to distance herself from Mrs. Vess's increasingly proximate chin.

"All right, the girl's lips are sewn shut," Mrs. Vess murmured and proceeded to wink, mascara lightly smearing on her cheekbones. "I'll guess then, and you'll just say yes or no. Fair game?"

"Do you know all the boys in our grade, Mrs. Vess?"

"Of course, silly girl."

Florence sighed quietly. She turned her head sideways. The clock behind her said 1:09. She turned her head back again and sighed again, louder. "All right."

"That's my girl. Hmm, let's start nice and generic. Mason?"

"Mason Burr?" Florence repeated incredulously, her eyes wide. "Isn't he dating Sophia?"

"Oh."

"Yeah." She smiled with an air of finality.

"So that was the reason, I presume?" Mrs. Vess continued, voice sympathetic. "That he started a relationship with someone else?"

"I'm sorry, *what*?"

"Dear, it's okay to admit your feelings—"

"No, Mrs. Vess. It's not Mason."

Mrs. Vess looked at Florence, eyes quickly scanning her face. Florence looked right back, still smiling yet arching her brows.

After a few seconds, the counselor gave in and leaned back. "All right, not Mason. Who else? Patrick?"

"No," Florence answered, giving a side-eyed glance to see if Mrs. Vess would continue asking her follow-ups.

Mrs. Vess, surprisingly, did not. She simply moved on, as if checking off items on a grocery list.

"Don?"

"No."

"Jack?"

"No."

"Rupert?"

"No."

"Lee?"

"No."

"Samuel?"

"No."

"Nate?"

"No."

"Michael?"

"No."

A pause. Mrs. Vess seemed to have used up all the names on her list and propped her chin on her hands, brows furrowed intensely like a referee looking for subtle fouls. Hesitantly, Florence picked up her white water bottle to take a drink.

"Ah, I got it!" the counselor suddenly declared loudly, jumping up so quickly that she almost flew off her red-and-yellow office chair.

"Mmhm?"

"Finneas!" she announced.

Florence spat out her water.

Mrs. Vess looked smug. "So I got it!"

"Mrs. Vess, please—"

"Come on now, honeypie," she continued soothingly, "body language doesn't lie. Now tell me how it started, and we can start the healing process, okay?"

"Mrs. Vess—"

"Florence." The word sounded final in the counselor's mouth, and though her smile was still plastered on, one streak of sunlight hit her bushy hair, adding an almost regal, certainly intimidating look.

Florence felt the streak of sunlight across her chin, probing her to glance at the clock. It was 1:18. She wiped her mouth with the back of her hand, paused for a moment, and finally answered, "AP Lang class."

"Go on, darling."

"I, uh, was partnered with him for a project, and he was just so considerate and, uh, friendly that I couldn't help . . . liking him?" Florence described, her voice remaining perfectly neutral.

"Tell me what you like about him," pushed Mrs. Vess, looking as if she was fully invested in the story.

Florence thought for a moment. "He's . . . tall, and seems quite athletic. His scores are decent, but he also participates in extracurriculars a lot, like robotics. He has a lot of friends.

Also, he has a nice nose." She said it almost too quickly, and then quickly bit her lip. Alas, Finneas Pinnock was an art student, and never once participated in a robotics event.

But if Mrs. Vess knew, she didn't show any skepticism on her face. In fact, the counselor was close to tears, her eyes focused intently on the student before her. "Florence, that is very, very wonderful and I'm so, so happy for you," she gushed, hands wiping tears furiously.

"Urm, thanks, Mrs. Vess," Florence answered happily, and sat up a bit straighter, as if preparing to stand up.

The counselor leaned in closer. "And what did Finneas do recently that caused . . . all of this?"

Florence scrunched her face a little. "Oh, Mrs. Vess, he didn't have anything to do with the breakdown. It was the six APs and 2 IBs plus all the yearbook committee drama, but I'm working on it now."

"Psssh, sweetie, don't lie," laughed Mrs. Vess, waving her hands dismissively. "Those courses had always been there, from the beginning of the semester. There must've been something, right? Something that caused the breakdown at that precise moment?"

"Ma'am, I don't think there's a need—"

"Honey, you can tell me anything—"

"No, really—"

"Ms. Chandler." Silence. "That boy did something, yes?" The counselor's tone was stern, her eyes narrowed.

Florence looked up. The sun was piercing directly through the window, angled toward her. It hurt her eyes a little, and her vision blurred temporarily.

It was almost as if she zoned out for a second, surrounded by a familiar warmth that covered up her lanky frame like molten gold. Somewhere, deep inside of her, strings of a memory weaved in and out of existence, its colors mapping out Finneas's fingers ripping a piece of paper littered with her distinctive scrawl.

She felt her chin nodding.

That was all Mrs. Vess needed. "Aw, darling," she let out, teary again, "I'm terribly, terribly sorry that happened. It must've hurt, didn't it?"

Florence nodded again, her whole body collapsing on the cobalt-blue armchair. She almost wanted to remain there in the sunlight, eyes chasing the fleeting patterns it made on the walls and brain's jagged edges eroded away by the brilliant metallic waves.

"I'm sure he liked you in his own way," the counselor continued gently, earning another nod from Florence.

"Now, just know, there are so many worthy candidates out there, who might be even more attractive than Mr. Pinnock, all right? I adore him with my heart, but boys like Patrick. Or Nate. They're some of the best, darling."

"Yes, Mrs. Vess."

"You'll be lucky one day. I know you will."

"Thank you, Mrs. Vess." Florence felt the fuzziness in her mind decrease, and soon her eyes saw blue tints again, trace of thought jumping to the next thing she wanted to say.

She sat up a little taller, and slowly asked, "I also wanted to talk to you about the SAT—"

"Oh, dear," the counselor chuckled, "You don't need advice on that at all. You'll ace it, as usual."

"But I—"

"Honey, what are you even worried about? I'll be very much surprised if you don't get a 1600," she teased, tone light.

"All right, Mrs. Vess," Florence sighed, and leaned back again.

"With you, just . . ." Mrs. Vess paused a bit. "Just listen to your heart a little more, okay? Don't deny your feelings. See the world in all its love, and the richness that comes along with it."

Florence smiled, tight-lipped so she wouldn't laugh outright. "I'm sorry, Mrs. Vess, but I just think there's too much going on in my life. When you have grades and activities and extracurriculars and competitions and friends to also pay attention to, love really isn't a priority, you know?"

Mrs. Vess looked straight at her, the sunlight illuminating every curl. "Everyone has a space for love in their lives, sweetie," she said quietly, enunciating every word. "In fact, life would be freezing and boring without it, don't you think? I'm sure you've experienced it, with Finneas?"

"Finneas?" The word sounded foreign on the girl's lips, a piece of candy she never quite remembered popping in.

"Finneas." A small vision of golden and the freckles of the boy's cheeks.

"Finneas," Florence repeated, and she suddenly was overwhelmed by a wave of emotion, its threads like sunlight and its destination the AP Lang classroom two doors next to the staircase on the second floor.

"Yes. Now go out there, and show them who owns the school," Mrs. Vess declared and stood up. Florence mimicked her movement. The counselor stepped forward to give her a large, enveloping hug that resembled melted alloys.

"Learn how to love, Florence," she whispered, voice muffled.

"All right, Mrs. Vess," the girl answered.

Florence didn't check the clock until she was halfway across the building, and only when she looked at her phone did she realize it was 1:40. Five minutes until class.

"Florence, where were you?" yelled Bridgette, pacing down the hall with a cup of cold coffee in her hands.

"Had a meeting with Mrs. Vess," Florence answered, and her own voice sounded muffled. She barely grasped the coffee given to her.

"About what?"

"My crush on Finneas."

"You have a crush on Finneas?" asked Bridgette incredulously. A few people slowed beside them and inched closer.

"Oh well, it was buried, yet she brought it out, clear and square."

"Do you even know Finneas?"

"Not really, it's just . . ." Florence stopped for a moment, her smile suddenly dropping, then picking back up a millisecond later. "I just have this feeling, you know? Thanks to Mrs. Vess, I know I like him now."

Bridgette stood there and stared at her friend for a few moments, then shook her head and whisked them off to IB French.

Days later, news was circulating around St. Barbara High that the notoriously private and aromantic Florence Chandler had a crush on Finneas Pinnock, who was now dragged to the robotic club by his friends.

The students forgot about that one small calculation mistake in Calculus class a week ago that led to Florence sobbing for over an hour, her hands still writing down the notes vigorously even as the droplets of tears stained her paper. Love was the answer. Love was always the answer.

And whenever someone walked up to Florence to ask her why she liked Finneas, she would never respond directly. She would just wink—mascara lightly smearing on her cheekbones—and say, "It was always there. Mrs. Vess just found it for me!"

Immortals

I.

Welcome to the land of the immortals, the hill upon the clouds, the palaces built from every exquisite element of the world. Open your eyes and gawk at the crowns constructed from raw diamonds, feasts filled with jars of ambrosia, pillars speckled by stardust. Feel the roar of fire, the crackle of thunder, and the spring of water beneath your feet.

Welcome to Olympus.

You must have heard the tales of the gods and goddesses, most likely from nanny years ago at bedtime, the worn stories repeated over and over again until your eyelids drooped. You must have learned the names of them all and forgot them soon after, the strange combinations of letters replaced with math equations and scientific terms. You must have loved the myths of ancient times once.

Zeus, Poseidon, Hades. The three brothers controlling the three spheres of the world. Apollo, Ares, Hephaestus, Hermes, Dionysus. The five gods who fooled the mighty and wooed mortal women. Hercules, Perseus, Odysseus. The countless heroes that battled every evil and brought good to all humankind.

Yet the goddesses are restless, their cheeks rosy from anger or excitement; perhaps both. They circle you, young traveler, one voice on top of the other, speaking of events long gone and forgotten by mortals.

So take out your pen and paper, fragile human. Because the goddesses will not wait for anyone. They've been itching for this moment for the past thousands of years.

Welcome to Olympus, where told tales take tantalizing turns.

II. Hera

They must have told you that I am easily angered.

By my disobedient children, by the childish whims of my siblings, but by none so much as by the mistresses of my unfaithful husband.

Yet they did not tell you about my husband, did they?

They did not tell you how we met.

I was the last one to be taken out of our father, Cronus. I remember stepping out into the sun, my eyes unadjusted to the sudden brightness and vividness of my surroundings, and in the middle stood a young man who was too much of everything. Too toned arms, too bronzed face, too wide smile.

The smile doubled when he saw me.

"Hi, sister," he drawled out, voice slick with what he may have thought of as attractive, yet which caused bile to form in my throat.

I did not pay much attention to him. A new world was presented in front of me, painted with shades from every color of the rainbow, its existence drawing me in.

He did not stop. He came to my house every day, with fresh flowers from the valleys across the ocean and fresh words complimenting my beauty. He promised me power, devotion, and love, his earnest eyes shining with excitement. And, of course, the time where he transformed into a cuckoo bird in order to draw the words "I love you" out of my mouth.

To say I was untouched is hiding the truth. When a man tells a naive girl they would rule side by side until the end of time, she believes it. I allowed him to take my hand in proposing marriage. I allowed the oaths to be said, the guests to be delighted. Perhaps I even allowed myself to imagine a future with him, a close-knit family overseeing the prosperous earth.

It was five months before he started to hit me. Six before he started seeing other women.

I do not know if he bruises them like he bruises me: the fury of lightning against my scalp, the well-trained fists slamming into my delicate back. If he makes up for it after, with a kiss on the cheek and ambrosia by the bed. If they forgive and forgive until their hearts run dry.

I try to tell them to run. To run as fast as they can. I send demons and curses after them so they stop handing themselves to him on a glass plate—so fragile, so easily shattered.

They tell you I am vengeful, young mortal. Yet, in all honesty, the anger has burnt out thousands of years ago, leaving only the ashes of bitter pain floating around in my ageless body.

You see, I am the goddess of marriage. Young girls pray to me on their way to dance galas or during the middle of their wedding ceremony or right before they give birth. They pray in hopes that my love would bless them, would carry them through.

As if I have an ounce of love left in me for marriage after the shambles of my own.

III. Athena

I am the goddess of wisdom, human. Perhaps not so coincidentally, I also get sculpted with armors and spears, helmets and shields, daring anyone to come closer to the fountain of knowledge.

They portray me as if I am devoid of emotion and color, as if my intelligence erases all and any parts of my femininity.

That might be true now, after centuries and centuries of solitude. But I was once young too.

I was once in love too.

She was called Arachne; how lovely is that name, with rolls and soft edges but also hard consonants that leaves you breathless.

She was a shepherd's daughter, her nails usually chipped and slightly dusty, which left faint fingerprints all over my cheek. Even after all those years I can still see the precise blue of her irises if I close my eyes: they were the exact shade of the Mediterranean Sea during the hottest days in July.

I wish I could say that I proclaimed my love to her, that I promised the golden arches of Olympus to her every night we laid together. Yet it was far from that, and to describe it as anything otherwise would be changing our story.

We were two women navigating their way in a land where a woman's hand can only be held in a man's. I was young, and vain, and scared, the words she deserved always hanging at the tip of my tongue. So I never said them and instead took us on wild trips across the summer islands of Greece, her body intertwined with mine. I gave her the most extravagant gifts, the rarest fineries, all so her heart would stay with me.

It did, until they found us.

Or, more precisely, they found her. They found the jewels on her vanity, the smell of seawater in her room, the intricate weavings right outside her door. The weavings we did together, my fingers guiding hers and the summer sun freckling her too-frail body. They marveled at the woven images, voices loud as they called toward my palace in Olympus, asking for a contest between me and my beloved.

"The best weaver."

As if I was second to anyone.

As if I would allow her to lose anything.

I bent my needle and used all the wrong colors of string; it was hard to weave anyway, with her presence so close to mine like the center of gravity. She won, naturally, her eyes crinkling up into the smallest of smiles.

I thought that would be the end. The foolish mortals would leave us alone.

Yet it brought her fame and attention, all unasked for and unwanted. Villagers marveled at her from her morning visits to the well to evening outings carrying dirty underclothes to wash. Suitors piled up against her door and asked her father for her hand in marriage. Eventually they became impatient and offered so many riches that the shepherd was keen to accept it.

She ran to me, cheeks stained with tears, begging me to take her away. We could go anywhere, she told me. As long as we were together, she wouldn't mind a thing.

I looked at her, my beautiful lover, her fragility laid out on my hands. And I looked toward Olympus, where affairs needed to be handled and decisions needed to be made.

I felt my heartbeat thrumming against the burning ambrosia within my blood.

I smiled at her and told her I could not.

I turned her into a small little creature, so the men could never find her. She could make her own home, capture her own prey forever. I promised her that it was for the best, that weaving and forgetting was better than being stuck with an immortal, with no trace of years on their faces as you slowly fade away.

So Arachne became an eight-legged spider, and she wove every single day without my guidance, the delicate webs almost a mockery to my purposefully thick knots. I wonder if she had forgotten me. I wonder if I wished her otherwise.

And as her descendants roam the earth, free of any ties with the divine, I sit in my palace, the armor and shield protecting my heart from ever getting touched again.

IV. Demeter

It is not wrong to love your daughter, mortal.

I am sure that your parents loved you, whether it was wholesome or deranged. And I am sure you love them back, although you might not admit it.

My Persephone was born on a soft spring day, with sakuras blooming and dandelions floating around her. It was so different from the night of her conception, which was all dark stone walls and cold winds through alleyways and the hands of the ruler of gods grasping my shoulders forcefully. The birth of my baby erased all my bruises, nightmares, and uncertain hands that often traced my abdomen, leaving behind only joy at her fingertips.

I vowed to the oceans that I would protect her with all I had.

She grew up in a sheltered environment, playing in the creek and picking strawberries and wrapping wildflowers around vines. I made sure there was no danger around her, that my daughter would be the goddess of spring forever, her innocence and purity coloring the world in the most pastel shades.

She was out with the nymphs, simply wandering around the valleys, when Hades took her.

Hades, my ugly, slimy, cold-hearted brother, took my baby girl with a sweep of his hand and dragged her to the Underworld.

He threw the flower into a jar with no water. He forced the light to fade out in the dark pits of the dead. He kissed the untouched lips, beard scratching the thin skin of his bride.

His bride. A bride that never agreed to marriage, nor to being forced to live in atrocious conditions for the rest of eternity.

I was furious.

The earth felt my rage. Crops shriveled, hearth cooled, and flowers withered into forgettable pieces of ash; storms shook the plains of the mortal world like an extension of my hoarse voice. They prayed to me desperately—the mortals—and begged for the famine to end. They asked for spring to come again and the plants to grow once more.

Yet how could spring come when the goddess of spring was locked up underneath their feet, her wings clipped and her hands tied to Hades' filthy throne?

Nothing would come between me and my daughter. Not the world, and certainly not my scrawny brother.

Eventually he got bored with stripping my daughter's dignity, and Zeus convinced him to let Persephone go.

I saw my girl running toward me that day, her lips stained with the burgundy juice of pomegranates, her eyes clear and bright despite the horrors of the past months, her skin no longer sun-kissed but pale, and felt peace at last.

Eros was praised when he ran away with Psyche; they called it true love. Apollo and Daphne's story was sung across parties; they said he was devoted. Yet old, selfish Demeter had no right to chase after the one she cared about most.

It is not wrong to love your daughter, mortal.

Nor was I in the wrong to love mine.

V. Aphrodite

The first thing you think when you see me is about beauty, isn't it?

They created sculptures of my body, paintings recreating my face, poem after poem surrounding the charisma of the goddess of love. They tell you that Aphrodite, with her plump lips and flawless skin and sultry gazes, is gorgeous.

Love is many things, mortal. It is attraction and lust, but it is also devotion and tenderness, loyalty and balance, rationality and hope. I govern the love not only of body but also of the mind and soul.

Yet when you've been told, over and over again, that you're beautiful and nothing else, beauty becomes all you're worth.

For centuries, men have stripped me down to nothing but the outline of my figure; I became the symbol for seduction and desire, the face of short bursts of passion. They act as though the only thing I do as the goddess of love is to flirt with anyone with an inch of masculinity—whatever men desired at that moment, protruding muscles and broad shoulders or sharp cheekbones and husky whispers.

I am not here to defend myself, human. I have tried to, time after time. Yet when all a woman's known for is her sexuality, your words drown out to be the faint hum of white noise while they continue to objectify everything you are.

So I will admit to all my sins.

Perhaps I was a flirty young girl, my charisma taking the lead before my thoughts, the world too full of opportunities for me to resist. Yet a compliment is not a permission slip to my body. A glance is not an invitation to a full-fledged relationship. Every touch and comment is justified by my appearance and my charm; every thumbprint on my body was somehow caused by the body I was born into.

Perhaps I was an unfaithful wife, but I am not the only unfaithful Olympian. The ruler of Olympus himself has had more mistresses than all the goddesses combined, yet he remains the symbol of masculinity and power. The god of the sea slept his way through the islands of the Mediterranean, yet they praise him to be a great father the moment he cared slightly for one of his many illegitimate children.

The gods of Olympus are not punished, ridiculed, and condemned for the affairs they have. Yet my love is seen as promiscuous and unimportant—as if the goddess of love could not love properly.

Perhaps I am driven by my emotions, the passion I have for romance dominating the choices I make while helping humans. Perhaps I grant wishes too easily and do not understand the full weight of my powers. If the people I've helped are happy and satisfied and in love, I become happy. They often forget that I live and breathe intimacy: between lovers, between family, and with oneself. The gift of love is so delicate yet so meaningful; I cannot limit myself and only grant it to the selected few powerful enough to gift me fineries.

I am done being the villain, mortal. It is fine if they vilify me; they always find ways to vilify beautiful women who know their own beauty. Yet they have to hold their precious men to the same standards. They have to spit at Zeus, whisper stories about Poseidon, and tear down Apollo if they want to spit, whisper, and tear down me.

Tell them to burn the witches, for witches have been told they're witches from the moment they exited the womb.

But burn the warlocks too.

VI. Artemis

When I was three, I hunted down my father, Zeus.

What a father he was, a man whose characteristics I've heard from everyone except himself, since he had been absent until then. I knew I was a bastard child, an unwanted offspring produced with half a thought from him and no approval whatsoever from my poor mother. Yet I took a bet, and decided to ask him what he long owed us.

I found him by the creek on a mortal island, his ageless face untroubled and his skin an almost glowing bronze. I heard later that he had just turned one of his nameless lovers to a goat in order to prevent her from giving birth.

"Father," I said loudly as I walked up to him. I recall him looking surprised, as if I was the first girl in his life to confront him like this. Perhaps he had a thought of striking lightning on me right there, so I didn't grow up to be trouble.

I must've looked pleasant enough, so he didn't.

One of the many mistakes he's made in his life.

"My darling Artemis." He gave me a toothy smile. "Why are you here?"

I felt then that I would not be able to stand this man for long periods of time.

So I told him my six wishes.

They were not bad, in my opinion: to never, ever get married; to have a fine bow and arrows made by Cyclopes; to have more names than my wretched brother, Apollo; to release light to earth; to have sixty nymphs as my servants and friends; and to roam in the mountains forever, unrestrained and unaffected by the chaos that would soon unfold around me.

Somehow, he agreed to all of them. I must have been a persuasive speaker, because it was a day after that when all six wishes were granted, and I was free to live them out for the rest of eternity.

I am not frequently mentioned in your folktales, traveler. And I have no desire to, since to be mentioned meant interacting with the rest of the fussy, obnoxious Olympians.

I came back here to tell you a secret that is not really a secret, mortal.

Why did I ask those wishes?

Because for the past thousands of years, hunting with women is more freeing than living with men will ever be.

And it is up to you and the rest of your kind to show me that I am wrong.

VII.

You have certainly overstayed your welcome, mortal.

The gods were happy, yet they have gotten bored of your endless inquiries and foolish assumptions. Finish up your drink. Escort yourself out of the palace. Travel downwards, until your feet are not upon clouds but rooted in firm earth.

But before you leave, take one last look at Mount Olympus in all its glittering glory, for this will only appear in your dreams henceforth.

Turn your head so you do not see the goddesses burning gaping holes in your back with their gazes. There is no need to flatter yourself, human. If you fail, they will simply summon another lost traveler with bright eyes and a pen in his pocket.

They will wait forever for the exact right tales.

And they will stand here, unmoving, until you vanish out of sight, once and forever.

Expectant. Pessimistic. Hopeful. Broken. Immortal.

The Heaven Express

1.

"One minute until departure. One minute until departure."

The speaker's voice was an instantaneous chord of static that temporarily deafened Eleanor Bradbury's ears. Of course, she knew it was because her hearing had been decreasing ever since she reached her sixties, but Lord knows she'd be in her grave before admitting that.

Or perhaps not. Being dead was not a welcome thought to her.

"Billy, dear, what do you think of the champagne?" she asked her husband, who sat beside her and had eyelids almost completely closed. He bounced right up when she said his name.

"The perfect ratio of bubbles to liquid, sugar to bitterness. You have to say, the Heaven Express serves some damn good champagne."

Eleanor watched as he took another drink and smiled sheepishly at her. Apparently, the alcohol was already kicking in. *Lord*, she thought, *maybe I shouldn't have encouraged him to get champagne off of the service menu.*

Smiling as politely as she could, she tapped twice on the left of her seat. Immediately, the two glasses of champagne fell to a spot perfectly perpendicular to the handle and disappeared.

"It's moving!"

"Look, it's moving!"

Casting a look that resembled laser beams to the source of the voices, which turned out to be a group of poorly dressed individuals all crammed at the back of the carriage, Eleanor peered outside and saw the spotless green lawns blurring into one another as the train picked up speed. The sign above her started to light up softly:

"WELCOME TO THE HEAVEN EXPRESS, MS. ELEANOR & MR. WILLIAM BRADBURY!"

"Excellent service attitude," she muttered absentmindedly to an already-asleep Billy as the city of Atroxia disappeared behind them.

2.

"Two kids?!"

"Shush, Gab, everyone can hear you."

Gabrielle Lopez clamped her mouth a little too late and received another glare from the stern-looking woman sitting a few seats in front of them. God, who angered her today? Knowing they were the same age—the Heaven Express was only for people aged 65—gave Gabrielle a headache. She didn't want to be associated and generalized with people like *that*.

But maybe she was just extra energetic today because she was with her schoolmates, some of whom she hadn't seen in more than forty-five years. All the rumors of the Heaven Express's journey and destination seemed so silly until she saw a familiar redhead the moment she stepped on the train.

"Carl!" she had yelled.

He had turned back sharply, and they had stared at each other for a few seconds before embracing, the rhythm of the engine's sound dancing like the decades long lost between them. After that, they started to scan the platform for classmates, and it wasn't long before the whole class was assembled at the back of the carriage, so different yet so similar to their past selves.

Emma, who still hummed absentmindedly but coughed often; Randy, with his tie fastened neatly and his thinning hair; Tiffany's insistence of sitting like they used to do in schoolrooms and the subsequent realization that they forgot almost all the seating charts; Mario helping everyone with their luggage, yet fumbling ever so slightly with his cup of tea; Druella's stories, laced with the claps and gasps long due.

And Carl, with his usual air of confidence, expensive-looking cigar in one hand and a half-filled beer jug in another. And her, of course, Gabrielle, the loudest in the room, the social butterfly, who used to be known as "Carl's Gabrielle."

They sat tentatively next to each other only after everyone else was already seated, far from the days when all they wanted to do was stick their heads together to read an adventure novel or trying to poke the other more times than either could count. And no one dared to make fun or sing that childish old rhyme of "Carl and Gabrielle sitting on a tree, K-I-S-S-I-N-G" or even bring old memories up, for they knew that Carl's wife passed away just a month earlier, narrowly missing her voyage on the Heaven Express.

His wife.

Who wasn't her.

The dull ache in between her ribcage forced her back to reality, back to the conversation on Steve's family. "The science whiz got married and had two kids?" she said in a quieter voice, squeezing out the most convincing smile possible.

Steve grinned embarrassingly, and the rest chuckled along. Mario clapped Steve loudly on his back, saying something along the lines of "shouldn't have teased you back then about being single forever" and sounding a little too friendly, just like he used to before coming up with a worse trick. Soon, the back of the carriage exploded again with Mario whispering something inside Steve's ear, to which Steve reacted with a fake punch. Chants of "fight, fight" rose as Steve and Mario laughed alongside the noise. A petite woman walking by almost jumped in terror as the crowd booed.

Carl suddenly spoke, his baritone voice reminding them of their age despite the small pushes Steve and Mario were still sneaking to each other. "How are your children doing?"

"Fine," Gabrielle answered a little too quickly, and then elaborated with an involuntary pinch of her nose, "Mary just delivered her second baby last year. Mandy seems to be settling down in the countryside, but with her, you never know."

A soft sigh. "Of course, she takes after her mother."

"Hey!"

"Just kidding." He smirked at her, and suddenly all his wrinkles disappeared and his eyes turned bright, and they were just the same as they always were. The two plain yet stubborn kids always giving their teachers a headache with their never-ending chatter and paper airplanes thrown across dusty back corridors.

But they hadn't been children in a long time, so she forced herself to ask, "And I hope your children are doing well?"

His eyes returned to their muddy state, the wrinkles deepened themselves, and he took a long swig from the half-empty beer jug before answering, "They're adults, they can cope."

"As they will gracefully. And you?"

"Coping too, although not as gracefully as them."

Silence. She forgot how to speak for a few seconds.

"I'm terribly sorry, Carl. I know I said this in the virtual meeting, but—"

"I know, Gab. Thank you."

They didn't speak another word for the rest of the train ride.

3.

"Please wait while the halls are converted into tables for your convenience. Lunch will be ready shortly."

Natalie Lee didn't wait for the speaker to finish before stealing another glance at the woman slightly to the right of her. She first noticed her when the train started to move, and the light reflecting off of the familiar curls caught her attention. All of a sudden, her youth came crashing down on her, all in the form of a name:

Alicia.

Alicia.

Alicia.

Maybe the curls were white, unlike the color of hazelnuts in her memories. Maybe the once-full lips were now wilted like rotten roses left on the sidewalk. Maybe the eyes were no longer filled with beaches and light and her.

But her Alicia was still there, and somehow, that was enough.

The sharp profile remained the same, as well as the addiction to coffee. This was how they had always treated their emotions—hidden to escape execution.

Until...

"Natalie?"

Natalie started, and found Alicia suddenly in front of her, eyes wide.

"You—"

"I—"

"We—"

"It's been—

"—A long time."

The two stared at each other, unsure of what to say, or how to comprehend the existence of each other after all those years.

"Have lunch with me," Alicia finally said after a few seconds of tense silence.

Natalie laughed, then suddenly wondered why she did. "Of course, Alicia, of course."

And so they sat around the newly formed round table, waiting as the conveyor belts brought dish after dish.

Alicia broke the silence again. "Where's your husband?"

"I never married," she answered quietly, aware that two women dining together in a carriage full of couples was novel. "Didn't want to lie to anyone, or myself."

A chuckle. "Same. Although I'm quite surprised that you didn't; you've always been the more traditional one between us."

"Well, if I was truly traditional, there would be no us," Natalie bit back, strangely offended.

Alicia's grin dropped for a split second, but before anyone else caught on, it was back in place. "Of course, how dare I accuse the good girl of being too good. You've always been brave, Natalie, and now I know that hasn't changed."

The truth laid in between them: In Atroxia, or actually anywhere in Divumus, the act of romantically being with a person of the same sex was punishable by death, since one wasn't able to produce offspring that way. And staying single in a city where almost everyone was married off was the quickest way to cast unfavorable attention on yourself.

"I changed a lot, Alicia," she replied.

"Not in the places that matter."

Natalie wanted to scream at her former lover. She wanted to prove that she was older and wiser and less naive; less likely to run off with beautiful girls with eyes laced with stars to coastal towns and live in a fantasy for ten years and have it all break with the death of her parents. She spent decades in a law firm, having only colleagues and never friends. She became rich and powerful, someone her old self looked up to. She was better, in every way.

Except one.

"Do you still love me, Natalie?" Alicia whispered, and even though not a soul heard except for the two of them, Natalie still felt more exposed than she had ever been.

Words stuck in her throat, itching to get out yet scared to make contact with oxygen.

How could she pretend in front of *her*?

She finally breathed. "Yes."

4.

The wine glass shattered, earning several surprised yelps from neighbors. A trash can—or was it a robot?—came to clean up the mess immediately.

Pam Laurent could hear, distantly, her friends telling her to stop, to just "take a rest from drinking all that goddamn wine," to look at them. But, as she had never once done before, she ignored them.

"The Heaven Express?" she sputtered, her tongue twisted and numb with alcohol. "They're getting us to heaven, all right."

She could picture in her mind vividly the posters right before its first voyage, back when she was still a child. Minimalistic, bolded words promising the "journey of a lifetime," only accepting elders aged 65 or older. A few years after that, attendance became mandatory for all elders in the country, and the year after, only individuals aged 65 could go on.

That was because the Heaven Express was a one-way train.

No one ever came back.

At that point, rumors started going around Atroxia about where the destination of the Heaven Express actually was. Some said it was a reclusive Scandinavian village where all could live to be one hundred years old. Some said it was a fraud, and elders were sent to a mine where they dug for gold until they dropped dead. Still others said that there was no destination at all, and the train just went on. Forever.

Siblings, children, grandchildren had all tried to contact their family members who went on the Heaven Express, sending their letters to all corners of the earth or requesting virtual meetings with the government. Yet no response was ever received.

She had asked her mother one afternoon, "Where do you think the Heaven Express leads to, Mama?"

"Do your chores," was her mother's answer.

And so Pam did her chores and studied hard and married early and had three children and stopped herself from crying when she signed the divorce documents and raised her children to be sensible adults and gave everyone around her everything she had, but deep inside, she still wondered.

Yet there was no answer, even when she was on the Heaven Express herself, ready to meet her destiny, suddenly realizing that the majority of her life was spent not living for herself but for the wary smiles of others.

She broke.

"Pam, stop, you're making a fool out of yourself!" A sharp voice, probably belonging to Hannah.

"And why would you care?" Pam yelled, her head dizzy and turning the room into an abstract, colorful, thousand-year-old oil painting of the Renaissance. "Why would I care? Why would anyone care, if life is the preparation for death, if no one will remember us anyway, if the fate of humankind is destruction?"

"Pam, what the fu—"

"Ms. Pam Laurent, please return to your seat in thirty seconds, or we will be forced to arrest you."

"Arrest, arrest..."

And for some unknown reason, she started to laugh hysterically, even when her friends forcefully pushed her back to her seat. She laughed at the faces of people around her, believing they were about to be saved. She laughed at the white pristine carriages of the Heaven Express, built so magnificently yet so typically, as if the government couldn't spend an extra minute on coming up with a new design. She laughed about the land of Divumus, where everything was scientifically advanced to a point of complete automation and civil and peaceful and beautiful, except when you have a dangerous idea or if you've lost your usefulness through decades of giving and giving but never receiving.

She laughed as she woke, as she opened her eyes for the first time, but most of all, she laughed in defeat.

5.

Winona Singh leaned against the window, trying to get as wholistic of a view of her surroundings as possible. In her left hand was a pocket-sized, leather-bound journal open to a page almost filled with words, and in her right hand was a fountain pen with its tip slightly overflowing with ink.

A glass of freshly squeezed apple juice, which was starting to oxidize, remained untouched.

"Clouds . . . grass . . . sun . . ." she muttered, appearing to be completely isolated in the middle of a carriage filled with happily conversing people.

Biting the nib of her pen, she started to document using the same scrawny handwriting as before.

"It's 1:45 p.m. Sun still shining as previously mentioned, although clouds seem to be drifting in opposite direction as the train; presence of large plants is starting to decrease, while grass and wildflowers remain constant."

She lifted her head again, thought of something, and wrote,

"Train appears to be completely self-driven, and no person other than the passengers is present. Perhaps individuals will greet us when we arrive at destination."

When she looked up again, there was a brief pause in her head's motion. Then, the residue of excitement and longing vanished, leaving only a widened pupil of onyx. Her eyes not moving once from the window, the pen in her hand scribbled quicker than ever.

"Something glinting about ten miles ahead. Seems to be strands. Danger?"

Before the last word was written, the pen dropped onto the floor.

6.

The Heaven Express rolled merrily on its way, unaware of its surroundings and never once losing speed, even when the tip of it touched the almost invisible net of atomic strands, the distance between each strand half the atomic radius of a standard hydrogen atom. Each strand was also designed to replicate a laser cutter, although precise to the distance of the nucleus.

And the tip simply ... disappeared.

The rest of the train continued, sliding gracefully into the now sixty-year-old net that the Prime Minister of Divumus unofficially named "Dreamcatcher." The countryside field swayed slowly against the soft wind, oblivious to the screams of old men and women as they watched their partners fade into thin air. Near the sole tree of the field was a small sign, with Divumus's motto printed cleanly upon it:

"The greatest happiness of the greatest number is the foundation of morals and legislation." —Jeremy Bentham

A gentle lilt of the bird broke the quietness while the Heaven Express turned into nothing, its end finally colliding into the net and vanishing out of existence.

And so the atoms of the honorable guests of the Heaven Express, carried by gusts of tender wind, started to float upward, welcomed by the warm, hospitable sun as they sought the path to heaven.

Dowager

I.

October 1st, 1867; Imperial Palace

She rose at six in the morning, awakened by the sound of faint chirps, most likely from the ibises in the imperial garden. As soon as she laid her hands on the mahogany drawer, the curtains opened, revealing young Ming Yue, all ribbons and stutters.

"Your highness, good morning." A low bow, head almost touching the ground.

She didn't speak for a few moments, enjoying the tension in the room.

"Fetch me some water."

Ming Yue bounced up (too eager), bowed again, and exited the room, only to return just seconds later with an ornately decorated china bowl filled to the brim with water.

"For your highne—"

Tap.

She flicked Ming Yue's arm lightly and fought the urge to smirk as the servant twitched dramatically, spilling water all over the silk bedsheets.

"Ming Yue!" Sounding stern was surprisingly easy, given the absurdity of the prank.

"Your . . . your highness, I'm extremely sorry," the girl stuttered, scurrying off to find a rag.

The pale sunlight of early mornings slanted through the window and reflected off of the pool of water in front of her, creating picture upon picture of ancient folktales that paraded around her walls. The monk, the monkey, and the pig. Liang Shan Bo and Zhu Ying Tai, their graves next to each other. Mistress Meng, her tears splitting open the Great Wall itself.

Swish. She swirled the water, making the images blur together until all Chinese folklore were one giant story on loss and love and doing what's right.

And then Ming Yue bustled in again, two clean rags in her hands and eyes slightly red.

"I'm sorry again, your hi—"

"Don't do it again," she warned without a lilt in her voice, but she allowed the servant girl to clean up her bedsheets and satisfied herself with the sweet dew of Han Lu.

"Does your highness want your usual breakfast?" Ming Yue asked timidly, taking the now-empty bowl. She bothered to nod, even though the stupid servant asked it every morning.

"The blue one," she said before Ming Yue had the chance to inquire (as usual) about her robe for the day.

"Of course, your highness."

A rustle in the room nearby, and the servant returned with a delicately sewn dragon robe of royal blue, a small vermillion purse necklace, and black silk shoes with an elevated concave heel. She surveyed each piece as it was laid gently beside her. Formal yet not overdressed. Powerful without looking assertive.

Perfect.

Ming Yue helped her into the robe, although she needed no help. The firm fabric clung to her silk underclothes, and she needed no reflection to tell her that she looked as regal as the first emperor of Qin when he set thousands of texts ablaze. Although it was a shame that she could never directly see herself in the bedroom. Mirrors in the bedroom were considered bad luck, and the previous emperor made sure she was in the room with the best feng shui, which meant nothing that would bring her the slightest of bad luck.

"Does your highness feel comfortable in the attire?" Oh, how repetitive the servant girl was.

"Yes. Now go fetch my breakfast," she replied, tone a bit harsher than she expected, but it was effective. The girl disappeared again.

She slipped into the shoes herself. For some reason, she did this every morning and always felt better when her own hands dug into the heels, her own body bent to adjust the fit of the tip. If she could put on her shoe, she thought, she could do anything.

She was independent, even more so than the emperor. She could do things that he couldn't: like putting on one's own shoe, for his bloated belly and chubby fingers could never allow him to do that.

The servant returned to announce that the breakfast was already in the dressing room, and she allowed herself to be led through the short hall connecting the two rooms. She smelled the deliciously soft scent of steamed rice cakes. Sure enough, she saw the bamboo steamer filled with fried rice cakes, predictably filled with sweet red bean paste. Next to it were a dozen or so dishes, ranging from pickled vegetables to sautéed shrimp (with their shells removed) to a bowl of porridge.

Decent.

She sat down on the chair, and Ming Yue started to style her hair as she ate.

The servant first brushed her hair with a walnut wood comb, then, with slightly shaking hands, constructed a bun low on the back of her head—almost like a sparrow's tail. Then the headdress, its iridescent pearls draped on the sides slowly clinking as Ming Yue gradually lowered it onto her head and fixed it with pure silver pins covered in flowers of various shades of red, all matching with the largest flower on the right side of the headdress. It was the most in style right now, because she started wearing it.

A few more flutters, another added necklace, and the girl stepped back. "I am done with your hair, your highness."

She gently put her chopsticks down and didn't miss the glance of pure longing Ming Yue gave to her unfinished plates. "I will get started with the day, then," she drawled. "And girl, finish the dishes for me."

The servant's eyes lit up in joy, and she bowed hastily before moving forward easily. It was the greatest honor to eat one's master's food.

She smiled. Just a little. No one was there to see, after all.

II.

The jewels clanked in the mahogany box, and her wrists suddenly felt free. A faint red mark was etched along the place where the dozens of bracelets once sat.

Ming Yue was taking off her hairpins, dead silent. This was unusual; the girl liked to talk and would often chatter away during the evening routine. Yesterday the servant asked her about how the daily briefings of national events proceeded.

She replied with a gaze that caused the girl to quickly drop on her knees with apology. But it was familiar, hearing the youthful voice talking about the most ordinary things in life, her slight accent rolling over some vowels and speeding through consonants.

She glanced up. There were faint tear streaks under Ming Yue's eyes. There was nothing in her knowledge that happened. And it was inappropriate of her to ask.

But she felt a slight twinge in her heart; an unfamiliar and unwelcome presence.

So she began talking herself. "When I was young, my mother would teach me how to distinguish ripe watermelons. In fact, she took me to the market herself."

Ming Yue glanced up, her dimple showing again. "Really, your highness?"

"Yes," she answered. The headdress came off, and suddenly she was filled with memories of busy cobblestone streets, the cool air of Beijing's summer, and the pungent smell of garlic that was strung together and held on poles. "She went up to a watermelon, lowered her head until she was almost touching the fruit, and tapped slightly with her index finger. Like this." She mimicked the movement, finger stretched out, and imagined the black stripes of a watermelon in front of her. "There was this particular sound, clear without being echoey, that meant a perfect watermelon. She tapped around the whole stand, and I thought she was crazy, crouched like that." She chuckled uncontrollably, then immediately stopped.

The servant didn't seem to notice and nodded eagerly. "My mother taught me that too, your highness. Although we didn't have enough money to buy watermelons, so I never actually tasted one," she remarked, voice trailing off.

She looked at herself in the mirror (the sole chance she had before returning to the bedroom). Thirty-one, skin mostly still soft to the touch, mouth pressed into a thin line that was slightly too slanted to belong on her otherwise youthful face. They told her she was a beauty; she wondered how much of it was true admiration and how much was fear. "They taste sugary. And full of water. I don't like them that much," she said after a moment. "I would much prefer litchi. Also a summer fruit, yet so much stronger in flavor. My mother used to order them every week."

"Your mother seems like a wonderful woman, your highness," Ming Yue whispered.

Her hair was being combed. "Not exactly, girl," she murmured, the aftertaste of plum wine suddenly bitter in her mouth. She felt a thousand needles prickling her scalp, and an image condensed like the air on autumn mornings.

The sky, brimming with tears.

"You should be honored by this opportunity, stupid girl."

"Mother, I am not ready, I'd like to read more—"

"Reading gives you nothing but rags."

The air was too stuffy; did anyone open the windows during the morning?

"That's enough," she snapped to the girl, and stood up. Ming Yue quickly led her back to the bedroom.

A cup of pearl-dust tea was waiting by her bedside table. It was warm, which normally suited her taste, yet made her feel even hotter right now. She hastily called away the servant (and the cup), and tucked herself in.

That night, she dreamt of the monk and the pig and Mistress Meng and watermelons and her mother. She jolted awake when her mother appeared hazily, cold sweat on her back.

The chimes outside indicated midnight.

She stayed awake until dawn came, and it was time to rise again.

III.

150 Years Later; Eastern Mausoleum

"Everyone, gather up here, please!" the tour guide shouted into his handheld microphone and waved his flag as individuals wearing caps and uniform yellow t-shirts crowded around him. The sun was blazing overhead.

"As you have probably heard from the locals, Empress Dowager Cixi was once buried right . . . here," he pointed at a certain spot in the seemingly ordinary soil, "with several other emperors of the Qing dynasty, such as Kangxi and Qianlong. Cixi is arguably the most famous, due to her notoriously lavish lifestyle, corrupt political behavior, and huge spending habits that ultimately led to the dynasty's fall."

A little girl poked her mother. "Mama, is Cixi the woman you told me about yesterday before bed?" she asked.

The mother caressed her daughter's hair lovingly. "Yes, darling. Remember what I told you? Empress Cixi was a very, very bad woman, and you must learn knowledge and be kind to others in order not to end up like her."

The girl widened her eyes and nodded.

"Again, quite famously, this area was looted by warlord Sun Dianying and his men in 1928, which caused Cixi's body to disappear," the tour guide continued, already moving away from the supposed burial site. "If we continue this way, we can clearly see . . ." His voice started fading as the crowd followed his steps, backs turned to the wooden caption board that contained a picture of Cixi in her mid-fifties.

"Pearl-dust tea! Pearl-dust tea! Buy a pack for your friends and family!" a faraway voice announced. "Used by Empress Cixi herself!"

The sunlight passed through the crowds of people and fell on the dirt, illuminating the tiny speckles of new roots that added some much-needed green in the bleary neutral background.

Yet hundreds of feet underneath, her rotting body stayed in the dark.

Day's Dozen

[7:30]

It was not the shrill sound of the alarm clock that woke her up but the sound of her cat scratching at the foot of her bed (again), its nails on the hardwood creating the most unpleasant type of rhythm. For a few seconds, she stayed unmoving, her vision pitch black and her mind still wandering in the hazy forest of previous dreams. But then she remembered what day it was, and she quickly jumped up.

The good thing about small apartments: The bathroom was so close to her bed (and everything else) that she barely had to spend any time in the chilly January air with her paper-thin pajamas before welcoming the lukewarm embrace of her towel heaters.

Two minutes for teeth and two minutes for face; serums and creams, powders and matte lipsticks—today's shade was burgundy. Her hands slipped and poured a bit more foundation than desired, while the concealer tube seemed to be running out.

Breakfast was on the tiny counter: a cold bagel with cream cheese wrapped in plastic, as usual. It went down with two vitamin pills and water that tasted suspiciously like rust, yet the clock read 7:44, meaning she was most definitely going to be late.

Not today. Any day but today.

She burst out the door, toes still wiggling into beige heels.

[8:30]

The subway flew past familiar buildings and strange new billboards as she shifted slightly, one hand clutching the steel handle despite its iciness and the other religiously cupping a cup of scalding coffee (caramel macchiato, low-fat milk).

She knew Shanghai's winters were not particularly cold compared to her friends' snowball fights in New York or the three feet of snow in Toronto. Yet she couldn't help but grit her teeth as the metro door opened and the crowd shifted her out, bare ankles meeting frosty wind.

Why did she wear heels again?

[9:30]

The receptor machine scanned her face twice before letting her in, which almost caused her to not get on the elevator. Her fingers found the seventh floor button, even though they were clammy and numb.

She noticed the woman next to her, pearl on top of cashmere, lean slightly away from her; maybe the perfume was too strong (her heart ached a little for the kuais she spent on the new Lily of the Valley scent).

Clanks against the metal floor, as the familiar yet consistently aggravating elevator music faded behind her. *Why did they always play Für Elise, its cliché half-notes descending in a scale of almost mockery?* On the way to her cubicle she purposefully slowed down her footsteps when she passed the manager's office.

One, two. One, two.

She waited and prayed for the sparse auburn hair to rise above the walls. Yet everything remained silent.

Sighing to herself, she walked on.

[10:30]

The coffee was cold before she got to take the first sip.

She closed the half-filled datasheet, legs stretching until her knee hit the cold wood surface of her cubicle. Perhaps it was time to stand up and walk around a little.

And see if Gorilla would finally call her in.

Gorilla was actually Mr. Yang, but she didn't think he deserved the sunshine-bright last name; in fact, the moment when she walked in the office ten months ago for the interview, his overgrown mustache and beady eyes gave her an idea of exactly what to call him.

Come on, don't call him that when your fate is literally in his hands—a Gorilla can't promote you, but a Mr. Yang can.

"Leslie!" someone called, voice tucked deep into their own cubicle. "Can you help me retrieve the documents, darling?"

Shoot.

"Of course," she answered, and forgot to take her Lotus cookie on the way back.

[11:30]

She was halfway through typing the report when a sticky note was placed on her table.

Meeting at 2.

Looking up, her caramel eyes met with cold hazel. Almost instinctively, her cheeks rose for a smile, even though Samuel Gong was the last person she wanted to smile at right now (or any time). "Hi, Sam, how's your day?" she heard herself ask.

He did not smile back, and his elbow—covered by a spotless blazer—wedged comfortably on the edge of her cubicle. "Finish the report before the meeting," was all he said before turning to leave, clearly expensive leather shoes (that shine imitated Gorilla's forehead) clanking obnoxiously.

As if he knew her heart was racing for the promotion results. As if he was already celebrating his victory and laughing at her consequential failures.

She bit her lip. Three quarters of a year, and she'd already raised the sales of her department by 3 percent. Surely Gorilla, with all his primal instincts, could smell the burning potential in her.

Tilting her head back for another swig of coffee, she found the cup empty.

[12:30]

"And he smirked! Smirked!"

Karina was waving so dramatically that a fry almost flew into her face. She dipped her chin protectively and took another bite of her Caesar salad. It was the third day of her supposed "diet week," and flashing images of mint-chocolate-chip ice cream from the shop just outside the office's back door had already filled every inch of her cells.

"Leslie, are you okay?" Karina now asked, body turning toward her. "I know you've been stressed lately about the promotion, but live a little, all right?"

"Of course." She grinned (hopefully convincingly) and poked at the chicken breast crumbles. It must be a miracle, how living humans could consume this horror and not die of a heart attack.

On the way out, she bought a cup of sweetened milk, its red-and-white packaging lighting up the interior of her black purse.

[1:30]

Two more pages of the report written and the pillow behind her chair was becoming increasingly comfortable. Maybe a little nap wouldn't hurt, since after all . . .

She opened her eyes.

1:55.

The report remained unprinted.

She sprinted across the office, the heels of her foot digging into the heels of her worst nightmares. Becoming temporarily religious when pressing the print button and whispering as many divine beings' names as possible must've worked, since the printer produced seventeen beautiful pages of numbers and words instead of the atrocious mess it spit out last time.

Someone (she swore she heard it) chuckled. It must've been Samuel.

[2:30]

It had been thirty minutes, yet Gorilla was still ranting about projected numbers of the next quarter's Marketing Department's consultation office instead of promotions.

Her linen shirt seemed too stuffy in the room, and she could feel small sweat beads form like a crown around her forehead. Out of the corner of her eyes, she spotted Samuel with his own stack of papers, back straight and expression perfectly composed.

Her dad beside the kitchen table, eyes crinkling with rare joy when she handed him her certificate of merit. "You're set to do grand things, Leslie," he told her. "You'll make me proud one day."

She silently tried to raise her head taller by squaring her shoulders.

Gorilla's voice droned on and on as she told herself that she would not be afraid. Yet her hands quivered almost uncontrollably as she handed in her report on the way out, head bent again as if preventing the light above from shining directly upon her.

[3:30]

Her head hurt a little; maybe it was from the three cups of office Americano she downed when making another data table, trying to erase the dryness in her throat by swallowing impossibly bitter drinks.

Samuel was conversing with a colleague a few meters away, the sound of his laughter making her vision blur like a deer in headlights, except the headlights were nothing but the oversaturated, modern paintings behind the printing machine, and she was about to become a manager, not, god forbid, a deer.

Her back against the bathroom stall door, hot tears streaming down her face and staining the test paper that contained fat red numbers of "89." And that was the only time she ever cried at school.

She stood up to get the fourth cup.

[4:30]

The sound of clocks ticking was a catalyst for her heart to speed up. She could smell burnt paper, its scent crisp in the air as Gorilla's office door remained closed.

They said it would come out today.

[5:30]

Gorilla's voice, right when she was about to press the elevator.

"Leslie Shu, come over."

A bob of her head, then the realization that managers never bow. "Yes, Mr. Yang," she answered, closing the door behind her with her sight staying fixed on the ground.

"You submitted an application for the Marketing Department's deputy manager, correct?"

"Yes, sir." *Stop saying the same thing, Leslie. You sound agreeable, timid, and completely not like a leader.*

"And so did six other people."

"I understand, sir." *Goddamnit.*

She focused her sight on the potted plant next to Gorilla's seat. It contained a golden edge and sloppy Chinese characters taped on the side. *Happy Father's Day.*

A bird cried in the distance, most likely calling its mate back before sunset.

"I'm sorry to inform you that you were not picked for the position, Leslie." Gorilla said it so calmly, so smoothly, without a rise in volume or a prolonged pause between syllables, that she almost thought it was a joke before the silence and the realization and the panic hit.

The tip of her tongue threatened to spew out a million little impromptu essays that would expose the countless hours of sleep she lost in the past week due to excitement, and the edges of her eyes became dangerously wet. Yet she still fixed her gaze below her manager, and choked out, "All right, sir."

"You'll do fine as you are. And, girl, look at me more."

She obediently looked up at him, trying to conceal the redness lining her iris. For a moment, his murky eyes seemed almost pitying.

And she ducked her head. And left the room she was so close to claiming as hers. And heard Sam's victorious howl as the elevator door pinched out the light right in front of the tip of her nose.

[6:30]

Her lids closed involuntarily during the ride home.

Her grandfather handing the stuffed red packet to her baby cousin while she sat and watched, the lone bill leaving her feeling so empty she might float away.

Two balloons her first love bought, yet nothing for her other than the stark memory of the two of them embracing in front of streetlights that blurred in and out due to her tears.

Laughter from the back of the classroom, following every sentence of her campaign speech. Ink dots splattered on her pristinely kept white backpack. Her face crossed out with sharp scissors on the bulletin board. Jokes her principal told her.

The man who her mother arranged for her to go on a date with, his clammy fingers inching closer and closer to her exposed collarbones. Slurring insults and shards of glass after she pushed him away.

Deepening wrinkles in between her father's eyebrows and the lack of joy in his eyes when he saw her last time before Lunar New

Year. The word "proud" thrown somewhere in the dusty cabinets of their old apartment, forgotten.

She was almost unwilling to wake up and find out that she rode past her stop already.

[7:30]

She stared at the knives in her kitchen intently, their sharp edges glistening in the not-too-bright flat. Moments later, the roaring red in her brain died down, and she moved to lie on her bed as she ordered Korean fried chicken.

The pills on her shelf were taken down, yet her fingers fumbled and turned before releasing the white deadly pearls back into their jar. Instead, she took out a hardcover notebook and scribbled with so much force that one page tore in the middle of a sentence.

She laid in an empty bathtub (which was the sole reason her rent was sucking money out of her pockets like a vacuum cleaner), feet on the faucet as if silently directing it to open and swallow her whole. The marble caused shivers up her skin and prevented beads of tears from forming.

She thought of the one award that was never given to her in fifth grade, the unfinished novels thrown out of her bedroom, the scars across her cheek from a push down the stairs years ago. She thought of the admission officers who smiled scornfully at her high-pitched voice and the babies of her friends chaining them to their dinner tables. She thought of promotions, silence, and death.

Yet all she did was turn on her alarm for 7:30 the next morning and slide into her bedsheets, curtains half-closed to reveal stars twinkling above her answering faraway reveries.

Sunlight, Seawater, Saliency

She was late.

Somehow, that was the only thought in Brooke's ceaseless mind as she stood on the hovering platform that looked out into the Pacific. Perhaps it could be described as a train station, although no one desired transportation that stretched tedium into hours now. In the most fundamental sense, you waited in stations, just like her pacing around the delicate edges that shielded her from nature's suffocating embrace.

Beneath her feet was what they once called Shanghai—they still did sometimes, mockingly, as if the infinite breadth of cerulean blue was representative of the metropolis whose skyscrapers ignited the darkest of nights and worried Wall Street bankers (although that, too, withered into a few lines in high-school curriculums). Brooke never developed a love for the city, being born long after its demise, but she knew from her mother that this was where she originated: her great-grandparents, the third generation of Shanghainese businessmen, fled from its wobbly earth to America's chemically infused paradise.

America.

She remembered her conversation with James Madison a few days ago; the Meetings were always in her memory, partially due to obligation and partially because she liked to reminisce about old cobblestone streets or overgrown ivy in her spare time. They were sitting in a dusty library, his notes barely legible and her voice drowned out by the sound of hoofs rushing by.

"How can one feign democracy when the town halls are grasped tightly by elitists not different from Britain's George III," he had muttered in response to her questions on the Constitutional Convention. Brooke knew then that the answer she sought didn't lie within her country's fourth president and stopped paying attention: her managers wanted affirmations, not skeptical remarks from a thinning man.

But now, as she waited for her Chinese counterpart to arrive in nose-chilling cold, she wondered if he was reminding her of the essence after all. What good would her mission do if the purpose she preached for was just a more pristinely veiled version of autocracy than that of her opponents?

Revelations failed to come, but a figure did. Brooke felt the thunder crackle in the sky before she appeared, black uniform on top of pale skin, dark brown eyes reflecting the strikes of molded light behind her. A messenger of the eastern empire; a shadow of herself.

She tipped her head, and Brooke found herself doing the same. Upon closer inspection, the woman carried a small red pin on her left chest: a peony flower, if Brooke had to guess. Something bold and blinding and brimming with centuries upon centuries of turmoil.

"Brooke Wong," she offered as introduction, extending her hand to meet the feathery yet shielding fabric of her opponent's glove.

"Lianyi. Lianyi Tian." The syllables rolled off the woman's tongue, smooth like the storm clouds drifting above their heads, salty like the seawater that seldom spritzed into Brooke's half-open lips.

"How was the trip here?" she offered, mind already swimming with possibilities; the sky in her peripheral vision blurred in relation to the subject in front of her, edges sharpened and ears ready to preserve every word about to come. She was here for one reason and one reason only—she told herself and tried not to think about long-lost lantern strings or the taste of braised pork, so sweet it was almost bitter.

"It was fine, thank you. Didn't expect the rain, but I guess it does provide a nice backdrop." Brooke tried not to ponder the connotations behind Lianyi's casual remarks. "I heard that Manhattan experienced a crisp summer recently. Is it true?"

Brooke wanted to laugh, if not for Lianyi's undisguised display of knowledge on her whereabouts then for the characterization of hundred-degree weather as "crisp." Perhaps she was trying to find ways of knowing America's current lackluster progress—not that *her* country was doing better, Brooke thought triumphantly. "It's true. In fact, I spent the most wonderful summer there. They do provide the best cuisine, I'd say."

Lianyi's lips twitched up, and Brooke cursed herself for mentioning food. A few years ago, Congress ratified a bill that banned the consumption of animals. Of course, the president, fountain pen in one hand and eyes solemn, cited the "great initiatives of our environmental movements," but she knew even back then the plant-based meat trusts threw billions of half-stolen money into every campaign.

"You don't have to be satisfied with America as you find it. You can change it. I didn't like the way I found America some sixty years ago, and I've been trying to change it ever since." That was Upton Sinclair. They walked side by side down the road, finding no choice but to breathe in Chicago's acrid air. "After all, food, water, and the last shred of human dignity . . . without them, who are we?"

Brooke still didn't know the answer, but she knew her tongue probably reeked of human-made chow and craved what Lianyi probably had every day—pan-stuck rice grown with beams of soft light in between callused hands. At least, that's what their posters exhibited.

Which seemed to be true as Lianyi spoke. "Well, if you have time, I'll certainly invite you over to Beijing. You might see for yourself there."

Beijing. Brooke's brain crackled with possibilities. "I'd love that. How is Beijing doing?" She tried to hide it with a beam, but couldn't push down the bubbling feeling of victory in her heart as Lianyi blinked twice, silence stretching like a thickening fog.

"Oh, it's great. Perhaps the air is a bit more dense in the winter, but we get by quite well. I presume Washington does too." When she finally answered, her thumb was enveloped by clenching fingers and her voice was like artificial honey, unnaturally smooth and lethally sweet. Brooke fought the urge to squirm with discomfort, the algorithms within her skull already unravelling what Lianyi seemingly meant.

The waves roared beneath her feet, distant yet proximal. She wondered how they felt, ethereal bodies being warmed again and again, stuck between the burning skins of earthly skeleton and sky.

Maybe they were like John Winthrop, who stood before the swath of barren land they would soon call Massachusetts, Brooke hidden among his grimy followers. "A city upon a hill," he had cried, hinting at the essentiality of staying true to morals while being observed. Perhaps the sea had long been the product of scrutiny since the Viking days, its spirit already frayed at the edges from embracing humankind even as they split open its flesh.

No matter what, it was lashing out today, and Brooke felt its fury within each of her bones. It had already been almost an hour, and they were not even close to discussing the circumference of the answer she was seeking.

Lianyi was currently making polite conversation on book recommendations. After the awkward pause surrounding Beijing, Brooke assumed she was advancing too fast and resumed back to small talk. But now, the shelves of information within her mind were quaking with frivolity and excess.

She decided to try again. "I've been reading a few books on environments myself, but I haven't found them to be enjoyable. Perhaps you have any insight in that field?" The tone she attempted was supposedly nonchalant, but the consonants rushed out too quickly and Lianyi lifted her eyebrows a bit.

Brooke cursed herself. It was foolish for her manager to scoff and tell her the "Chinese girl was no more than a long-limbed puppet." It was foolish of McCarthy and his minions to send back scientists like Qian Xuesen, knowing very well there was nothing he did to offend America but the color of his skin. It was foolish of her to fall back into the same mindset that led to this shenanigan in the first place—ignorance and conceit. Decades of patronization and something deeper, something with the exact odor that protruded out of the Chateau of Versailles four centuries ago.

When Lianyi answered, she sounded as cordial as ever. "I'm not a large fan of that genre, but I do like history books. I've got a few recommendations on Afghanistan. Korea, too. The same goes for you?"

They were dancing around it now—waltzing across humid jungles and blood-soaked dirt, but in some way acknowledging this hundred-year struggle of power and promises and paradoxical importance between two decaying nations. Brooke could see her silhouette nestled within her counterpart's pupils, and clearly she wasn't hiding her pleasure as she wished.

She tried to contain herself by listening to the steady rhythm of the waves. "Yes, I have always been interested in those myself, starting from elementary years. I remember my fifth grade teacher talking about this. She told me history is just an Archimedes spiral."

Lianyi's eyes softened a bit at that. "Like a seashell," she reiterated, and Brooke nodded. Almost instinctively, she looked out into the horizon, but she knew she would spot no marine life, here or anywhere.

"We always get more extreme, don't we?" Lianyi continued, cheeks neither lifted nor sagging. "My ancestors say it's the course of nature, that every species ultimately destroys itself."

Her words made Brooke recall the Meeting with Montesquieu—it was one of her firsts, and the managers told her to go back as far as possible since they were testing her ability. Therefore, her mouth was dry and her head a little cloudy as she walked with the Enlightenment philosopher alongside Bordeaux's peculiarly still rivers; his words, nevertheless, were etched into her that very moment up until now.

"Too often, nations lose liberty in a day, but its citizens and laborers toil with gold-threaded blindfolds for as much as a century before they realize what they've lost," he had remarked in a sullen way. He was somewhat of a sullen man, eyebrows drooped and lips permanently pursed together, and his way of near-inaudible speaking prodded Brooke to step closer.

"If I may ask, sir, nations are arbitrary and so are governments, but would you say the same for humankind as a whole? Are we all but selfish, myopic creatures?" She had worded the sentence carefully, scared of sounding too modern in streets stained with cheap ink.

Montesquieu paused for a moment, then murmured, "I cannot say for sure, child, but I must admit that we're remarkably short-sighted for intelligent beings, which surely alludes to the circulation of mistakes and slowly deteriorating morals."

Brooke had tucked the confession into her heart as some solitary prophecy, but Lianyi's words sound virtually the exact same. She wondered if there were similarities in between them, stale and waning, that they had never noticed.

"Your ancestor is very wise," she commented absentmindedly.

From the corner of her eye, Lianyi looked almost pitiful. "If I'm not mistaken, Brooke, my ancestor is the same as yours."

Brooke wanted to laugh. How, after decades of separating herself from the fat-headed cartoons inside textbooks, after an hour of wary suspicion, did Lianyi think that would make them somehow more comfortable with each other? Her internal notes and algorithms were screaming with impatience: Get to the point, and leave.

"Perhaps. I'm from Shanghai. A lineage of businessmen, if my grandmother was being truthful. You?"

"Hebei." For the first time since her appearance, Lianyi's eyes were filled with some overflowing emotion. Brooke couldn't tell what, but she did note the small traces of glimmer gathering in the edges of Lianyi's eyes and a sheer blush. "I haven't gone home in three years."

"Neither have I." Working in the government, with her particular occupation, prohibited Brooke from essentially living any sort of private life. She missed seeing her mother—checkered apron and fingers smelling like garlic—rush to the door every time she returned and inform her, with a chuckle, that dinner was ready.

A sudden homesickness shuddered through her spine, almost causing her to shake a little. She wanted desperately to speak Mandarin with Lianyi. After so much time apart from her family, its syllables were painfully robotic on her tongue the last time she had to greet a Chinese guest.

Her brain was scolding her, daggers cutting through thoughts, for getting off-track yet again. Perhaps that was what her eastern colleague was trying to attempt: coercing her to blurt out something within the corridors of faded memory and long-lost intimacies. *Get back to the question*, it probed.

Yet, even as she tried to muster up the phrases to attempt another inquisition, her reserves were empty. Instead, she meekly asked, "Is the job difficult?"

Lianyi stared at some point next to her right ear. "I wouldn't say it's hard, but it's . . . taxing. As I'm sure all jobs are. As I'm sure yours is too."

"Yeah." Brooke couldn't come up with a better response.

"Yeah."

Once again, silence surged in between them, but instead of its previous scent of nervous sweat, Brooke whiffed in the lightness of Lianyi's perfume, citrusy and raw. They were still facing each other, and she could see her counterpart's salient nose slightly scrunched, as if preempting another obtrusive question. In some way, she wanted them to stay that way—two girls who could almost pass as twins, pins oversaturated like retro bulletin boards and names echoing similar bodies of water. Their feet were pointed toward the opposite direction of their countries, except it didn't matter because the world was drowning and evaporating and collapsing in a thousand other ways that even America, with all its promises of infinite glory, couldn't dream of preventing.

As usual, Brooke searched the Meetings for guidance: Jackson, Carnegie, or Lease. Metacom, Reagan, or MacArthur. But somehow, she knew, in between Lianyi's uniform exhales and the way the storm had ended without warning, that history couldn't save them; nothing could, not even artificially made meat or technology that carried well-read youngsters like her into obsolete days.

Perhaps not even Lianyi.

She looked up to catch the girl's unwavering gaze; Lianyi was too much smarter, Brooke had realized, and already foresaw the question. But she asked it anyway. "Lianyi, do they have a solution?"

The first ray of light pierced through the clouds and hit Lianyi's temple, almost crowning her. As always, her face was devoid of surprise, but if Brooke squinted hard enough, the small lining at the bottom of her lid could almost pass as tears. They waited for a second, half expecting a triumphant cry for some bird, but none came.

"No."

She didn't continue, and Brooke's mind was suddenly empty of follow-ups or reassurances or anything but pitch black. Lianyi turned away, eyes closed and hair billowing slightly, and opened her mouth again. "You?"

"No."

Somewhere, deep inside mainland China, a child must've lost their red packets, and their cries traveled like a shattered star's corpse, all the way into her eardrums. Or, it was Brooke's imagination, for children would not reach eighteen before dying alongside everyone else, so there was no point in giving them money.

There was nothing more to say between them, but somehow, neither made the gesture to leave. Instead, they stood side by side, two sides of a rusting coin, and fixed their attention on the Pacific Ocean, for it will remain long after their populations' demise.

Sunlight had fully emerged at that point, carving the ocean into gleaming fragments and lining clouds with the ghost of shadows. The horizon, untouched by brilliance, ebbed away. For a split second, it was almost as if the sky and the sea had converged, forging a perpetual expanse of cyan that wrapped around the forgotten city, its embrace equivocally slaughter and salvation.

www.ingramcontent.com/pod-product-compliance
Lightning Source LLC
LaVergne TN
LVHW041638060526
838200LV00040B/1617